A Scottish Christmas

ALSO BY EMMA BENNET

a scottish christmas

Emma Bennet

Joffe Books, London
www.joffebooks.com

First published in Great Britain in 2024

Cover art by The Brewster Project

ISBN: 978-1-83526-819-3

For Chris. This one's for you in honour of you being one of my least annoying sons. I love you billions and millions. Mum x

CHAPTER 1

Rose lined up the elf-shaped pencil sharpeners on the counter in front of her, ensuring she kept a welcoming smile fixed on her face in case either a customer or, more likely, her boss made an appearance. She was definitely getting better at blocking out Noddy Holder screaming, 'It's Christmas!' on repeat, she mused.

She shivered and glared at the goose pimples forming on her arms. If Malcolm expected a grown woman to dress up for work in thin polyester as Disney's Queen Elsa, he really should be prepared to turn the heating up significantly. At least the long blonde wig kept her head warm.

It was a particularly quiet afternoon in the pop-up Christmas shop despite it being a Saturday and the first of December. There hadn't been a customer through the doors for half an hour now. It didn't help that the shop wasn't exactly positioned on the most salubrious part of the high street, but rather, where rent was cheap, down an alley in between a vaping shop and a tattoo parlour.

The shop was crammed full of what could only, but fairly, be termed Christmas tat. Goodness only knew where Malcolm managed to source all his stock. Those 'contacts' of

1

his that she'd met since starting the job a month ago definitely worked out of the back of vans and were decidedly shifty when asked if they could provide more of a particular product.

Rose resolved to wander around the shop to warm up and see if she could reorganise things a bit. It would also make her look busier if Malcolm got bored of watching daytime TV and ventured down from the flat he lived in above the shop.

She cursed her ridiculous outfit afresh this time for being far too long and cumbersome to effectively manoeuvre through the narrow aisles of the shop. She bent down to pick up a particularly glittery toy Santa that she'd knocked to the floor.

Mid bend, she heard a polite cough from behind her. "Excuse me," said a man's voice with a soft Scottish lilt. Rose jumped, knocking her head on the underside of a shelf.

"Ouch," she muttered, standing and rubbing her head through her wig. She turned and found herself faced with a broad, suited chest. She glanced upwards. The man who stood before her was the very definition of tall, dark and handsome, with slightly messy chestnut hair and a jawline so chiselled, he'd give Henry Cavill a run for his money.

"You appear to have lost your crown," he said drily, picking up and then handing her the silver plastic accessory which usually adorned her head during work hours.

Their hands touched briefly and suddenly Rose was no longer cold.

"Thank you," she managed to stammer, doing her best to pull herself together. Really, someone that good-looking shouldn't go creeping up on people unawares. It was completely disarming. She found herself adjusting her wig.

"My pleasure," he said, and looked away. But had their eyes held? Just for a moment? Or was she imagining it?

"How can I help you?" asked Rose, regaining her composure as she self-consciously placed her crown back on her head.

"I'm not sure," the man said, glancing around the shop. Disappointment at its offerings was written all over his face.

"Was there anything in particular you were looking for?"

"I have some Christmas events I need organising," he replied, carefully.

"I'm afraid that's not something we offer here, but we could certainly provide decorations," suggested Rose at her most helpful and customer-friendly. "What kind of events are we talking about? Are they for children or adults? Is there a theme? What sort of budget have you got in mind?"

"You know a lot about this . . . Christmas stuff and decorating, I suppose?"

"I guess so — and I used to work in event organisation for a while," Rose admitted.

The man's eyebrows raised before he glanced around again, then seemed to come to a decision. "Could you organise some events for me?"

"That isn't something we offer here," repeated Rose.

"But is it something *you* could offer?" he asked, his eyes now meeting hers. Rose felt her stomach flip.

"Um . . ."

"What's your name?"

"Rose. Rose Aldridge."

The man looked her up and down before seemingly coming to a decision. "How much do they pay you here, Rose Aldridge?"

Rose opened her mouth to tell him to mind his own business, but before she could he continued, "I need someone to organise the aforementioned Christmas events for me, as well as decorating my house and buying and wrapping gifts, that sort of thing. Come to work for me until Christmas Eve and I'll pay you triple whatever they're paying you here. Accommodation and food are thrown in. And use of a car, of course — you do drive?"

"Um, yes I drive." Rose focused on stopping her mouth from hanging open.

The man handed her a business card. "Think it over. I'll need a response within the next couple of hours. You'd need to catch a train to Edinburgh tomorrow and start work on Monday. My assistant would organise your ticket."

"Edinburgh?" Rose was utterly bemused.

"Yes, my home and business are in Scotland." He sounded a tad impatient. He'd clearly decided he'd sorted out his problem and was ready to move on with his day. "I hope to see you in Scotland, tomorrow."

And with that, the man turned and left.

Rose shook her head and read the business card: *Alastair Duncan. Duncan Enterprises.*

"I'm sure there's something you could be doing instead of standing around," said Malcolm's voice, making her jump. Usually she heard him coming down the stairs and unlocking the door from his flat into the shop, but Rose must have still been discombobulated from her meeting with Alastair.

Rose chose not to answer.

"It's been quiet today, hasn't it?" Malcolm stated, glancing around the empty shop. "You may as well get off home. I'll give you a call if I need you tomorrow."

"Oh right," said Rose. *Damn.* Being on a zero-hours contract meant she only got paid for the hours she actually worked. She was going to struggle with her meagre, minimum-wage pay cheque at the end of the month. Maybe she could see if there was any local bar work she could pick up . . . Then there was . . .

She found herself actually considering the option of taking Alastair up on his offer. But how weird would it be to travel however many hundreds of miles it was to Scotland from London to go and work for a guy she'd never even met and just for a few weeks . . . She shook her head at herself. Though she'd always wanted to go to Scotland. And Edinburgh itself was supposed to be beautiful. She'd heard there was a wonderful Christmas market there . . .

Grateful that the day, although cold, was dry, Rose removed her awful wig, freeing her own shoulder-length darker blonde hair and quickly changed out of her Elsa outfit and into dark blue jeans and her favourite oversized black cotton

4

jumper. She pulled on her boots and her coat, and wrapped a large red scarf around her neck.

What should she do with the rest of the day? It was now two thirty in the afternoon. Would any of her friends be free? Probably not, they'd all be at work or looking after little ones in some cases. She'd fallen out of touch with a lot of her closest friends, those she'd met at university, anyway. Seeing them go on to do what she'd so longed to just hurt too much.

She could catch a bus to the Tate Modern and check out the new exhibition there by a sculptor she was a fan of. She'd heard good things about it and had been meaning to go. She meant to go to every exhibition she made a note of . . . And yet Rose found herself taking the bus in the opposite direction to the gallery and heading back to her flat.

She opened the front door and dumped her bag on the hall table. The space was silent and felt as empty as usual.

Rose walked into the kitchen, filled the kettle and put it on to boil before opening up her laptop. She didn't need to recheck the name on the business card as she began googling.

Alastair Duncan was a big deal. His estate was huge, and he ran several businesses from it. Rose was soon down a rabbit hole. She couldn't discover much about Alastair personally, other than his age — thirty-four — just photos of him at various charity events looking as handsome as she remembered, but she found plenty about the estate he owned. It appeared he also happened to be a genuine Scottish laird.

Rose stared at a photo of some of Alastair's estate. Would she be staying somewhere on it? It was beautiful. Not that she was considering taking Alastair up on his job offer. That would be ridiculous. Anyway, she could get a phone call from Malcolm at any time with more hours for her . . .

She knew she should probably look for another job, especially as the Christmas shop would be closing at the end of December. It wouldn't be reinventing itself as a pop-up Valentine's Day shop until February, and she wasn't prepared to dress up as Cupid. Everyone had their limits.

She'd had so many jobs in the past eleven months, and none of them had stuck. Certainly none of them had paid anything like what Alastair was offering.

Remembering the kettle, she made herself a cup of tea and a ham sandwich. Malcolm didn't offer lunch breaks or anything as civilised as that. She usually picked at food she hid under the counter but she'd been in a rush that morning and hadn't taken anything with her.

The kitchen could do with a good clean, she noticed. Maybe she would do it after she'd eaten . . . But what did it matter? It's not like there was anyone else to see it.

Rose had lived her whole life in this two-bedroom flat. Just her and her mum, until her mum had become sick. The space held a lot of memories, but now being here just made Rose feel sad and oh so aware of everything missing from her life. She knew she should move; it was silly to pay rent on a flat with an extra bedroom she didn't need, but the thought was exhausting and where could she afford that would be better?

She finished her food and half-heartedly sorted through some post that had been lying around and wiped down the countertop. Her gaze returned to her laptop and the photo of Alastair still on the screen. What would he be like to work for? She guessed she wouldn't have much contact with him if she were to accept his offer. He'd have far more important things to deal with . . . Wait, was she seriously considering this?

She'd be hundreds of miles away from home until Christmas, but then again what did she have to be home for? And it wasn't like she had a lot of planning to do for her own Christmas.

If she stayed in London, she'd have to find another job. She couldn't make it through the month on what she was taking home from the Christmas shop. If she went to Scotland, she'd get an all-expenses-paid trip and would earn a lot more than anything else she'd be able to find on such short notice. Just her luck that it had to be another job involving her least favourite time of year though.

Taking a deep breath, Rose picked up her phone and dialled the number on the business card.

"Duncan Enterprises, Mairi speaking," said a female voice with a slight Scottish accent.

"Hi," said Rose, suddenly feeling incredibly awkward. "My name is Rose . . . I um met Ala— Mr Duncan today, and he gave me his business card . . ." She sounded ridiculous. There must be a better way to explain this.

"You're the Christmas princess!"

"Queen Elsa, actually," Rose found herself murmuring.

"Typical that Alastair wouldn't realise that," Mairi said with a laugh. "But at least he let me know you were going to call. I'm Alastair's assistant."

Rose breathed a sigh of relief as Mairi continued, "So I'm guessing you've decided to take him up on his offer?"

"I think so," replied Rose, cautiously. "It's just . . ."

"Completely out of the blue and totally random?"

"Pretty much."

"Yeah," said Mairi. "That sounds like Alastair . . . Usually we hire a company to organise events but this year Alastair has family coming to stay and he wants someone in-house to make sure things run smoothly. I mentioned this morning that he was going to struggle to find someone as he's left it so late. Alastair walked into your Christmas shop, thinking someone might be able to point him in the right direction, and apparently, you're the somebody who can do the job."

"That's not exactly what I said . . ."

"Well, Alastair seems sure you're the one for the role. He's had me draw up a contract for you. If you're happy with it and sign, I'll book you on a train to Edinburgh tomorrow and you'll start work on Monday morning. Alastair said he made an offer based on your current salary, but didn't actually know your current salary so I guessed and rounded up a bit. I hope you'll be happy with it."

Rose found herself telling Mairi her email address and ending the call. Seconds later, an email pinged into Rose's email account with the contract attached. Rose was being offered more like four times what she was earning at the Christmas shop — and that was assuming she was still working there full-time rather than having her hours cut so much. She'd not find anything else that would pay anything like what Alastair was offering for the next few weeks. And Rose had to admit her life was completely stuck in a rut. Maybe getting out of London for a little while would do her good, shake things up a bit . . .

***

Rose woke the following morning not feeling quite so sure of herself and wondering if she was making a huge mistake. She'd tossed and turned most of the night, worrying about what exactly she had signed herself up for. What if Alastair was some crazy, demanding millionaire who expected her to work all hours on ridiculous tasks? *You can always leave*, she told herself reasonably. London was only a train ride away. And Mairi seemed happy working for him so he couldn't be a complete tyrant, could he? And the pay was *really* good.

She returned to bed to drink her morning cup of tea and eat her toast, unable to stop looking over at her almost completely packed suitcases on the floor. For so long she'd had someone else to look after and think about. When that ended, she'd entered survival mode, going through the motions to keep her life going. It was time to do something different, to take a chance. As much as she was reluctant to admit it, she needed to get on that train to Edinburgh.

CHAPTER 2

A couple of hours later, Rose was scanning her e-ticket to get through the barriers at King's Cross station and onto the platform where the 10.23 to Edinburgh Waverley was waiting.

Last chance to bail out, she warned herself, but she continued onwards. She had a seat reserved and was pleasantly surprised to discover it was in first class. She'd never travelled first class before. Already she was ticking off new experiences. A porter helped her get her two large suitcases onto the train and stowed away and Rose made her way down the carriage to find her designated seat.

Her reserved place was one of four with a table in the middle. As she approached, she could see there was already someone sitting in one of the seats across from hers . . . Someone tall with chestnut brown hair. Rose's heart sank as she sat down and had her suspicions confirmed: she'd be travelling opposite her new boss for the next four hours and eighteen minutes.

Alastair looked up from the previous day's *Financial Times*. He nodded at Rose. "You made it then," he said, before returning his attention to the newspaper.

"I didn't think I'd be in first class," Rose said, feeling she ought to make some sort of conversation.

"Feel free to move carriage if you'd prefer," came the reply.

"No, no, it's great . . . I've never travelled first class before. I heard there's free food and hot drinks . . ." She let her voice trail off. Why was she babbling? She guessed she was worried she'd offended him, but doubted her babbling would help the situation.

"Everything you've heard is true."

"So you wear a suit on a Sunday?" Rose blurted out. *Why was she doing this?*

"I had a breakfast meeting," sounded from behind the paper.

Having checked and seeing no reserved sign, Rose placed her leather satchel down on the seat next to her. She began taking out the sketch-pad and pencils she carried with her everywhere she went, despite not having drawn for a long time now. Being stuck on a train seemed as good a time as any to attempt to get back into the habit which, up to eighteen months ago, had been almost as natural as breathing to her.

"You're missing your crown today. I'm guessing you don't always dress like a Disney princess then?" asked Alastair, lowering his paper.

"No, only on special occasions."

Alastair frowned. "Ah. That could be a problem. I thought Mairi would have explained . . ."

Rose was about to stand and make a swift exit before the train pulled out of the station when she noticed the look in Alastair's intense green eyes. Mischief was written all over them.

"You're joking . . ." She sighed.

"Yes," he said, with a grin that she reflected was far too fleeting. "You won't be required to dress as any Disney princess while working for me." He folded up his newspaper and took out a MacBook.

"That's good to know," Rose said. "And by the way, Elsa is a queen, not a princess."

"I can only apologise." Alastair looked at her, amusement evident as his gaze met hers.

"It's an important distinction." Rose blushed and fiddled with her pencils, breaking eye contact.

"I imagine so."

Alastair began working on his MacBook and Rose took that as a sign she should stop talking rubbish at him.

She was distracted from her analysis of her poor social skills when the train began to move. She felt a glimmer of excitement in her stomach at the adventure before her.

Rose opened up her sketchbook, turning it to the first page. She'd been given it the previous Christmas. She'd finally opened it a couple of days after the event, having returned home, heartbroken. Her last present from her mum. Goodness only knows how she'd managed to arrange the gift from the hospice without Rose knowing . . . And just like that, Rose's resolve not to think about last Christmas unless she was by herself in her flat, and feeling particularly sad and lonely, dissolved and a fat tear rolled down her cheek. She wiped it away quickly, giving a glance towards Alastair to check he hadn't noticed. He appeared to be just as absorbed in his laptop screen as before.

She chose a pencil and switched places with her bag, shuffling over to the window seat. The one thing that was almost guaranteed to take her away from her problems, for a little while at least, was drawing. Within minutes she'd entered her flow state as she took inspiration from the passing views to sketch whatever she felt like, allowing her body to become reacquainted with the rhythm and movements which had once been second nature to her, blocking out everything around her, including her handsome co-passenger.

She was finally brought back to the present with a jolt as she felt something land gently on her, sending tingles all the way up her arm. She glanced down to see Alastair's large hand on hers and instinctively pulled away before looking up to meet his eyes.

"Sorry, you were miles away," he explained. "Would you like some lunch?" He indicated to the lady waiting to take Rose's order.

Rose's cheeks flushed red. How long had they both been watching her in her trance while they waited for her to answer them?

"Yes, please," she managed, accepting a menu and choosing the first thing that caught her eye, the New York deli sandwich.

"Drink?" asked the server, wearing a professional, practiced smile but no doubt completely fed up with the ditsy woman she was just trying to get a simple lunch order from.

"A latte, please," said Rose.

The food and coffees were delivered quickly and Rose was grateful Alastair continued to be absorbed in whatever he was working on. It would be more than a little awkward to make polite conversation with him while they were eating. She'd been counting on the long train ride to get herself prepared for what was ahead of her and here she was sitting opposite her new boss, taking tiny polite bites and worrying she had bread stuck in between her teeth.

But after a few minutes, Alastair closed his laptop, took the lid off his Americano and said, "Tell me about yourself, Rose."

Rose was a little taken aback that he remembered her name; for some reason she'd assumed he wouldn't. Maybe he'd just been looking it up in an email from Mairi. He stared at her. Rather intently, actually.

"Anything will do," he said sighing.

"Well . . . um . . . I'm twenty-six . . . I've lived in London all my life . . . Worked in a Christmas shop until yesterday . . ."

"And how did you end up working in a Christmas shop?"

Was this some kind of test? Was she supposed to say she'd got a BA in Christmas Hospitality or something? Rose didn't want to lie but she also didn't want to be put on the next train back to London.

Honesty had to be the best policy.

"I sort of ended up working there as a bit of a stopgap. I took a career break for a while and now I'm working out exactly what I want to do."

Alastair nodded. "You seemed to know what you were talking about when it came to organising events when I spoke to you."

"Yes, don't worry," she said quickly. "I worked organising events for years during and after university."

"Is that what you studied?"

"No," said Rose. "I studied Art." She felt embarrassment wash over her as Alastair's eyes glanced over at her sketchbook. She breathed an inner sigh of relief that she'd closed it before stopping to have lunch.

Alastair took another sip of his coffee. "My aunt on my father's side is an artist. Watercolours. She's coming to stay for Christmas. I think the two of you will get along."

Rose nodded politely, already dreading potential evenings stuck talking to Alastair's elderly aunt for hours about her painting. And then being asked about her own art and having to either lie or admit that she didn't draw anymore. Not until a couple of hours ago anyway.

She was actually kind of surprised at herself for getting out her sketch-pad in front of Alastair in the first place. She guessed it was because he'd been so absorbed in whatever he was working on that he wasn't likely to pay any attention to her. But now that he'd stopped and was focused on her, she felt awkward.

She was glad when Alastair finally reopened his laptop and resumed his work, not that she felt confident enough to continue her sketching. She took her book out of her bag instead and settled down to read for the rest of the train journey. Every now and then she found herself glancing at her sketchbook though and smiling.

CHAPTER 3

Rose and Alastair exited the train together.

"May I help you with one of those?" Alastair asked, indicating Rose's suitcases and then, in contrast, his small holdall.

"Thank you," she answered gratefully. She did have a lot of luggage, but she was going to be in Scotland for three and a half weeks, and she'd heard it could get pretty cold. She'd packed every jumper and pair of tights she owned as well as some smart trousers and shirts for when she was in 'work mode' . . .

"There's a taxi waiting for us on Market Street," Alastair said, checking his phone. "It's this way."

Rose followed his lead through the station and out into the grey, drizzly December afternoon. She took in as much as she could of the city as they walked in silence to a black Ford Galaxy with a small woman who looked to be in her fifties standing beside it. "Duncan?"

Alastair nodded.

"The boot's open," the woman said, getting into the driver's seat.

"Thanks." Alastair opened the back of the car to put his own bag in before slotting the first of Rose's cases in alongside it. He relieved her of her second case. "Would you like to go in the front?" he asked, courteously.

"I'll be fine in the back."

"Okay, the doors are unlocked."

"Hi, I'm Louise," said the woman as Rose climbed into the car.

"I'm Rose. Good to meet you."

Alastair climbed into the front passenger seat. He was so tall he looked all scrunched up.

Rose wished she'd thought to sit behind Louise, who was far smaller.

"You can move your seat back a bit if you like," she said, "I've got plenty of room."

"Thank you. I'm fine though. You know where we're going?" he checked with Louise.

"Yes. Looks like it'll take about an hour to get to the estate." Louise started the car.

"That's right. It's south of Peebles." Alastair took out his phone.

Alastair was working and Louise was silent so Rose watched the changes in the landscape, enjoying seeing the city dissolve into countryside.

She felt her eyes close and tried to resist but failed.

* * *

"Rose? Rose, it's time to wake up." It was Alastair's voice.

Rose jolted awake. They'd stopped moving and Alastair was holding open the car door. Her stomach sank. How embarrassing. She surreptitiously wiped the back of her hand across her face in case she'd dribbled. It seemed she was in the clear.

"There are a few things I need to do before dinner," Alastair explained, a smile threatening the corners of his lips. "My housekeeper will show you to your room and answer any questions."

"I'm staying in your house?" said Rose, getting out of the car. It had got dark since they'd left Edinburgh behind and there was a chill breeze which made her shiver.

"Yes, didn't I mention that?"

"No." She shook her head.

"And Mairi didn't either?"

"Nope."

"Oh. I apologise. I assumed you'd be given this information. A large part of your workload will involve the house. I tend to work from home when I can, rather than from my office, so it made sense to have you based here. As you can see, we have plenty of room."

"You certainly do." Rose's eyes widened at the large building before her. She hadn't found photos of his actual house in her googling. It should have been obvious that his home would be impressive, but . . . wow. The sixteenth-century building was three storeys high and draped in ivy with numerous chimneys on its roof. There was a single storey addition on its left. Light shone through the windows on either side of the doors, but most of the other windows were in darkness. She gave up trying to count them all.

"Would you rather I found you alternative accommodation? We have some cottages on the estate, but the couple that aren't inhabited are in need of work and—"

"No, no, it's fine. Don't worry," said Rose. "It's not a problem. I was just surprised. As you say, it looks like there's plenty of room."

"You're quite sure?" asked Alastair, poised by the open boot of the taxi.

"Absolutely." Rose sounded far more certain than she felt. Would it be really awkward to be living with her boss? But it wasn't like they'd be stuck in a tiny house together . . .

The air smelt fresh and clean as Rose turned her attention back to Alastair's home. She wished it was earlier in the day and that she could see it clearly. The house appeared to be very remote. From what she could make out, only countryside surrounded it.

She couldn't begin to imagine having a house like this for your home.

Alastair thanked and paid the driver. A small, late middle-aged woman with grey hair and an apron around her waist came out of the house as the taxi headed off back down the drive to the road.

"Mrs Reed, this is Rose, our Christmas events organiser. Rose, this is Mrs Reed. I'll leave you in her very capable hands."

With introductions complete, he left them and walked to the house, going inside through the slightly imposing double doors and closing them behind him.

"Hello," said Rose to Mrs Reed shyly.

"Welcome, Rose. It's lovely to meet you. Let me take a case for you."

The front door opened and two black Labradors bounded excitedly out to make their greetings. Behind them came a very tall girl with long dark hair — she looked around eleven or twelve years old. The group was joined by another dog who came running from around the back of the house. Relief flooded through Rose at the knowledge that of course there were other people also living there.

Rose bent down to pet the dogs and was surprised to find the friendliest animal, and the one being the most demanding of her attention, had little horns — and was actually a small white goat.

Seeing her surprise, Mrs Reed sighed good-naturedly and said, "Yes, he's a goat. His name's Houdini because he escapes from wherever you put him. I'm not sure how he got out from his pasture now."

"He's my goat," said the girl, reaching the group. "And of course, he wanted to say hello. I bottle-fed him when his mother wouldn't accept him. Now he thinks he's one of the dogs," she explained, with a laugh. "Mrs Reed loves him really."

"Oh, do I?" responded Mrs Reed.

"Yes," confirmed the girl. "He's not allowed to live in the house so he's always escaping and coming to find me."

"He's not allowed in the house because he destroys everything and he should be with other goats."

"He'd rather be in my room with me," muttered the girl.

Rose remembered from her research that one of Alastair's businesses was run from the estate itself. He kept goats whose wool was spun and dyed and made into socks, hats and gloves which were, according to the reviews on the website, very warm and comfortable, as well as pretty pricey.

"Your father had a special shed made for him," Mrs Reed pointed out.

"Houdini hates being all by himself in a cold shed!"

The goat gave a bleat of agreement before wandering off to join the dogs who were sniffing around a large pot with some sort of ornamental tree in it.

"Your father looks after all his animals impeccably, as you well know. He's not cold!"

"He might be lonely though."

"You know he can go and be with the other goats if he wants to. It's just he thinks he's better than them. Which is why he has his own little paddock for when he's being annoying."

"He *is* better than them," the girl retorted.

Mrs Reed didn't appear to have an answer for this. She turned back to Rose and said, "Apologies, Rose, this is Mr Duncan's wayward daughter, Isla."

"Hello, Isla," said Rose.

"Hello! Dad said you're going to be organising Christmas for us!"

"That's the idea." Rose smiled at Isla's excitement.

"Can I help? I've got loads of good ideas . . ."

"Now, Isla," interrupted Mrs Reed, "Rose is going to have a lot to do for your father organising the Christmas events for his work. You're not to get in her way."

"Oh, I'm sure there are things you can help me with," said Rose, kindly. She was rewarded with a big grin from Isla.

"I can show Rose where her room is if you like Mrs Reed," said Isla. "I know you're in the middle of cooking supper."

"Thank you, that's very helpful. Is that okay with you, Rose?"

"It's fine with me," Rose replied with a smile.

"Houdini needs to stay outside though," said Mrs Reed, firmly. "Put him in his paddock and then you can help Rose take her bags to her room."

Rose looked like she was going to argue, but presumably, the set of Mrs Reed's mouth made her rethink.

"I'll just be a minute," said Isla to Rose, and she took hold of the collar around Houdini's neck and led him away, muttering darkly to him about what a terrible lot he had in life.

Rose followed Mrs Reed into the house, them each carrying a suitcase, and into a large, double-storeyed entrance hall. "Why don't you wait here for Isla? I'll be in the kitchen if you need me," Mrs Reed said, leaving the suitcase she held at the bottom of the beautiful central staircase. She headed off, presumably towards the kitchen, followed by the dogs.

Rose looked around the space, beginning to envisage how she would decorate it. It was large and elegant with pale walls, heavy with ornate cornicing and large portraits of very serious-looking people. A pair of antlers hung over the front doors. Somehow it didn't feel imposing. Maybe it was the little touches like the pair of shoes left by the door that made it feel a home rather than a laird's manor house.

The events she'd previously helped to decorate for had been in large halls or marquees, not divided up like the rooms in this house. She'd need a theme she could carry through all the rooms.

The front doors reopened and Isla walked in. "Houdini's in his shed," she said. "Let me show you to your room first. It's really nice. The windows look out over the drive so you can see anyone arriving."

"Thank you," said Rose.

She followed Isla up the wide central staircase, the luggage divided up between them. At the top of the stairs, they turned right and continued down a corridor lined with panelled doorways. Isla stopped at the third doorway on the left and opened the door.

"Here we go," she said, turning the overhead light on and throwing her arms out dramatically.

Rose stepped into the room. The bedroom was square and painted a pale, pale blue. Thick damask curtains in a darker blue hung at the huge bay window and there was an actual four-poster bed. There was an ornate pine dressing table against one wall and a large wardrobe against another. She thought servants were usually kept out of the way in the attic rooms. Rose giggled to herself.

"Do you like it?" asked Isla, anxiously, putting the suitcase she carried down by the bed. Rose placed the one she carried next to it.

"Of course, I do," Rose said. "It's gorgeous!"

"Good," Isla said, smiling. "My dad's bedroom is just across from yours if you need anything and the bathroom is down the corridor on the right."

"Thank you."

"Would you like me to show you around the house?" Isla looked so hopeful, Rose couldn't help but say yes even if she was feeling more than a little overwhelmed and could honestly do with some time to decompress.

"Let me take you to my room first." Isla led Rose back to the staircase and they continued to the corridor on the other side of the house. Isla's bedroom was similar in size to Rose's but with wallpaper dotted with tiny flowers. It also looked out over the front of the house. It was extremely pink and girly.

"What do you think? Isn't it cool?" Isla asked.

"It's amazing!" said Rose, honestly. "This would have been my dream bedroom when I was your age."

Rose was shown the bathroom she would use and they returned downstairs and said goodbye to Mrs Reed who was leaving for the day.

As it was already dark, Isla couldn't give Rose a tour outside, but she took her around the downstairs of the house. It was beautiful; full of fireplaces and big squishy armchairs with thick rugs on the floor and cosy corners perfect for reading in.

Rose tried to take in as many of the ornate details as she could as they walked and chatted and continued her earlier planning of how she could decorate the place. The high ceilings gave her lots of scope and she was determined to make use of the picture rails which ran around a lot of the rooms. A huge tree in the entrance hall would be the first thing she'd focus on.

The house was undoubtedly large and grand but not ridiculously so. She knew she could make it feel homely and cosy for the festive season.

Isla was showing Rose the impressive library with its perfect mahogany shelving and actual rolling ladder when Alastair, now dressed in jeans and a thick wool jumper, came to find them. He put an arm around his daughter and kissed her on the head.

"Are you two ready for dinner?" he asked. "Mrs Reed said it would be done around now."

"I'm starving," said Isla.

"Come on then," replied her dad.

She'd be eating with the family then, Rose realised with surprise.

Rose followed behind the pair, watching how easy they were with each other. She'd never known her father. He hadn't been interested when her mother told him she was pregnant, to the extent that he then disappeared and neither of them ever heard from him again.

She'd honestly never felt the loss; her mum had been a great enough parent that she'd never needed anyone else. But it was fascinating to her to see this young girl so comfortable with her father, who clearly adored her and, for possibly the first time, Rose wondered if she'd actually missed out on something.

She didn't like to ask where Isla's mother was; no one else had mentioned her so far. Maybe she was working late or was away for the weekend. Or maybe she'd be joining them for dinner and just hadn't been introduced yet.

That theory was put to rest when they went into the substantial country-style kitchen and Isla began laying the large scrubbed pine table for the three of them while her father pulled a tray of roasted broccoli out of the oven. Rose was surprised; she'd imagined they'd eat in the rather grand dining room and had been a little intimidated by the idea.

Rose felt like a third wheel watching the pair work together so seamlessly and was grateful when Alastair asked if she could fill a jug up with water and fetch some glasses from the cupboard.

The cottage pie and roasted broccoli that was served up a few minutes later were delicious.

"Isn't Mrs Reed a great cook?" asked Isla in between mouthfuls.

"She certainly is," said Rose with a smile.

"She's been with us since before I was born," continued Isla.

"You're very lucky to have her," said Rose.

"Have you got everything ready for school tomorrow?" Alastair asked his daughter.

"Yes, Dad. My bag's all packed."

"And your sports bag? You've got football tomorrow, haven't you?"

"Yep."

"Any problems with your homework?"

"I struggled a bit with some chemistry, but I sorted it."

"Do you want to go over it with me?"

"Nah, I'm good."

They finished eating and loaded the dirty things into the dishwasher.

"We usually make popcorn on Sunday evenings and watch a movie. Would you like to join us?" asked Isla.

"Oh, that's really nice of you . . ." began Rose. She couldn't invade their special family time any more than she already had. She'd never imagined that she'd be eating dinner with just Alastair and his daughter and that had felt awkward enough without her joining them for their family movie night.

Alastair swooped in to save the situation. "Rose is probably tired after her long trip. Why don't we let her have some time to herself, eh?"

Isla looked disappointed but Rose quickly said, "I am tired — but I'll definitely need your input into how to decorate the house when you get home from school tomorrow."

Isla's face lit up. "I have loads of ideas!" she gushed.

"We're not having a giant inflatable snowman outside the front door," Alastair said, mock sternly. "We've discussed this before."

"Oh," Rose said, pretending to sound disappointed, "but that was going to be the centrepiece of my designs!" She grinned, making Alastair smile. He looked quite stern a lot of the time, but when he smiled his whole face relaxed.

"That would be amazing," said Isla, laughing. "But I think my dad would stick a pin in that snowman as soon as he saw it."

"I'll bear that in mind," said Rose. "I'll head up to my room and unpack a bit before an early night, I think. Thank you for dinner."

"Our pleasure," Isla said, politely. "It's going to be so fun having you here." She came over and gave Rose a hug and Isla felt her heart melt.

"Good night," Rose said.

"Good night," replied Alastair and Isla in unison.

"I'm going to choose the movie," Isla said to her father, heading out of the kitchen.

"Is there anything you need before you head up?" Alastair asked Rose. "Please feel free to use the kitchen whenever you want, and let Mrs Reed know if there's anything you'd like got in for you. Tea and coffee are over here." He showed her the cupboard above the kettle. "Would you like a drink now? I'm going to make myself some tea."

"Sure, that would be nice."

"Camomile or regular?"

"Camomile, please."

Rose stood awkwardly while Alastair filled the kettle and put it on and was grateful when he broke the silence by saying, "Isla seems to really like you."

"I'm glad. I like her too. She seems like a great kid."

"She is, though she's twelve going on fifteen . . . do let Mrs Reed or me know if she's getting in your way."

"I'm sure she'll be a great help."

Alastair gave a little snort as he put teabags in two mugs and added hot water before handing one to Rose, handle first.

"Thank you. I guess I'll see you tomorrow?"

"Yes. How about we meet at nine in the library so we can go over stuff and you can get started?"

"Sounds good."

"Oh, and Rose?" Alastair said, as she headed out of the door. "The house can get quite cold at night. There are plenty of extra blankets in the trunk at the end of your bed."

"Thank you."

"I'll see you in the morning."

"See you then."

CHAPTER 4

When Rose came downstairs soon after eight the following morning, Isla was dressed in her navy-blue school uniform and just finishing off her breakfast. The kitchen was warm and smelt amazing, but Rose couldn't help noticing that Houdini was under the table.

"Hi, Rose!" said Isla, her face lighting up at the sight of her new friend. "Did you sleep well?"

"I did, thank you, Isla." Rose had actually had the best night's rest she could remember in a while. She hadn't felt the cold, despite Alastair's warning. She didn't sleep well at home these days, and she usually had trouble sleeping for at least the first couple of nights in a new place. She guessed it was because she was so tired from the long train journey. Or maybe it was just that the bed in her room really was incredibly comfortable.

She raised her eyebrows and signalled to Houdini.

"He's sleeping," whispered Isla. "Mrs Reed hasn't noticed yet."

"Hello, Rose. What haven't I noticed?" said Mrs Reed appearing from the pantry.

"How did you hear that?" groaned Isla as Houdini woke up and got up to investigate what Mrs Reed was carrying.

"Isla . . ." said Mrs Reed, sternly.

"I'll put him back in his paddock," Isla said quickly, taking hold of Houdini's collar and reluctantly leading him outside.

"Goats in the kitchen . . ." Mrs Reed muttered to herself before remembering Rose. "Can I get you anything for breakfast, or would you rather sort yourself out?"

Rose was grateful Mrs Reed gave her the choice. It would have felt very strange to sit and watch Mrs Reed make her breakfast when she was perfectly capable of doing it herself.

She never usually ate breakfast anyway, just a black coffee to get a burst of caffeine in.

"I'll be fine with coffee, thanks," she said.

"There's a fresh pot on the table." Mrs Reed gestured to a large cafetière. "Help yourself to a mug from the cupboard."

Rose poured her drink and sat next to Isla's vacated chair.

"It's a nippy old morning," Mrs Reed said. "Why don't you have just a little bowl of porridge to warm you up?"

Before Rose had a chance to protest, she found a bowl of porridge from a pot she now saw bubbling away on the stove put before her.

"Thank you," she said, not wanting to appear rude. She'd eat a little to be polite and then get rid of the rest when Mrs Reed wasn't about. She could never stomach breakfast. She gingerly put a small spoonful in her mouth. And wow! It was absolutely delicious. And so comforting.

"You can have some sugar or syrup on it if you must," said Mrs Reed. "But there is proper Scottish porridge, cooked on the stove and served with a sprinkle of good salt."

"How come you never let me have sugar or syrup?" Isla said, coming back into the room.

"Because it's not good for you. You eat enough sweet stuff as it is," Mrs Reed replied, firmly.

"It's delicious without anything added, Mrs Reed. Thank you so much," Rose said, not quite believing how much she was enjoying it.

"My pleasure. Right, Isla, if you're all done there, go and get yourself ready for school. We'll be leaving in five minutes."

"I'll see you later, Rose," Isla called out, leaving the room in a whirlwind.

"What happens with Houdini while Isla is out at school?" Rose asked.

"He spends the day annoying me is what happens." Mrs Reed sighed. "He has a large enclosure with a warm, dry shelter in the garden which comes up to the back door here. However, it seems to be that little terror's life purpose to escape and eat anything I've planted in the kitchen garden. When it's raining, I get calls from Isla at school wanting me to go out and check he's all right."

"Well, he is cute," commented Rose.

"And doesn't he know it," came the reply.

As if knowing he was being spoken about, Houdini appeared back at the kitchen door and bleated indignantly at Mrs Reed.

"I know it's time to go! I'm just going to get my coat," replied Mrs Reed, grumpily. Rose did her best to hide her smile at the housekeeper having a conversation with the goat she claimed she didn't like.

"Oh, and yes, he travels in the car with us to and from the school," Mrs Reed added.

Houdini waited, an air of impatience about him, while Mrs Reed put on her coat, whereupon he led her out into the hallway, his hooves clip-clopping on the stone floors.

Rose was left alone in the kitchen. It felt strange but it did allow her to have more of a look around than she'd felt able to before. She got the feeling this was very much Mrs Reed's territory and that Alastair and Isla, and presumably Isla's mother, wherever she was, were granted visiting rights with provisos.

She put her bowl and mug in the dishwasher. She still had half an hour before her meeting in the library with Alastair so she went back up to her room where she took her coat and a scarf and hat from her wardrobe. She'd unpacked and organised her clothes the previous evening before settling down in bed to watch art tutorials on YouTube.

She slipped out of the front door and looked out across the landscape before her. The temperature hit her immediately. It was absolutely freezing. Far colder than it had been in London.

The driveway led off into the distance, flanked on both sides by now bare trees which must be resplendent in the spring. Some goats were in a field to the right, and a small wood lay to the left. Even on this dull, slightly drizzly December morning, the view was beautiful. She didn't have a lot of time to explore but she pulled her coat tighter around her and began walking around the house, trying to get her bearings. She thought she'd worked out which was her bedroom window and which was Isla's.

The kitchen garden lay to the side of the house. It was obviously not looking its finest at this time of year, but there were still winter greens and the whole area looked well-tended. Maybe by Mrs Reed or perhaps by a gardener. *A garden this size must surely need a gardener*, Rose thought. Sticking to the path as her trainers were definitely not designed for the mud, she walked around to the back of the house where a stream ran through the lawn with its own charming little bridge over it, and the path split, with one section leading into what looked like a small orchard. She spotted Houdini's pasture and shelter, slightly incongruous by the back of the house. On closer inspection, she grinned to herself — it looked like a goat version of Fort Knox. How on earth he managed to escape from that was a mystery. Houdini must be one determined goat.

A tyre swing hung from the thick branch of a huge oak tree in the middle of the lawn, making Rose smile. If she could have been sure that no one would see her, she'd definitely have a swing on it.

She looked towards the rear of the house, wondering if she should go back in via the door to the kitchen, which would involve going through Houdini's enclosure, or the front. As she pondered, she thought she saw a figure at one of the downstairs windows. When she looked more carefully though, they'd gone.

She decided to make her way round to the front door so she could do a full circuit of the house. Her cheeks were stinging with the cold and she picked up the pace; she hadn't been moving quickly enough before to allow her to get warm.

Opening the front door, she pulled off her shoes and had just enough time to run up to her room and remove her coat, hat and scarf before going to meet Alastair in the library with a notepad and pen.

"Good morning," she said as she entered the library and found Alastair waiting for her.

"Hello," he replied. "Did you have everything you needed last night?"

"I did, thank you."

"And you're finding everything here, okay?" he asked tentatively.

"Yes, absolutely. Your house is amazing."

"And were you all right eating with Isla and me last night? It was only afterwards that it occurred to me that you might have preferred to have eaten by yourself, especially as it was your first night."

"It was lovely of you to include me. I just felt a little bit like I was intruding," Rose admitted.

"No, not at all. It's usually just the two of us rambling around here in the evenings. It's nice to have someone else to chat to. Not that I don't love talking to my daughter . . ."

"I get it," said Rose with a smile.

"Anyway, I just wanted to make sure that you're okay because . . . I saw that you were upset on the train yesterday. If my demands have taken you away from something, or someone, in London in the lead-up to Christmas I apologise. I know I can be a little too set on getting what I want . . ."

Rose felt her cheeks flushing bright red. So he *had* noticed her crying! "I'd hoped you hadn't seen . . ." she muttered.

"I'm sorry to bring it up. I don't mean to embarrass you. It's just, if you wanted to go back for a long weekend or something . . ."

"Thank you, but no. This is a wonderful opportunity and it's so kind of you to welcome me into your beautiful home. Honestly, my getting a bit emotional on the train had nothing to do with coming here. I'm happy to be here. And, frankly, I need the money."

"Good. I'm glad we've got that sorted out." There was still a hint of unease on Alistair's face.

"Shall we move on to the Christmas arrangements so I can get started?" Rose suggested, eager to move the conversation on.

"Sure. Christmas is a busy time workwise for me so I'm hoping that you'll be able to take over completely. I'm really not fussy about decorations or anything, just as long as everything runs smoothly."

"Sounds good."

"The most important thing is the two Christmas parties I need to host. One is for all the people who work for me on the estate, so that's fairly informal. Mairi, who you'll meet at some point, would usually hire out a restaurant for that and it's taken care of fairly easily. The second is for my business associates and potential investors. That's more of a black-tie event."

"My first concern is that I imagine most venues will have been booked up months ago, especially if you want to host on a Friday or Saturday. Haven't you left it a bit late to be organising a Christmas party?" asked Rose.

Alastair frowned. "The employee party will need to be on a Friday otherwise I doubt many people will turn up to work the next day. The more formal event should ideally be on a Saturday, which means invitations need to be sent out as soon as possible if we have a hope of people being able to make it. Funnily enough, some of us have things other than Christmas on our minds," Alastair said, shortly, before checking himself. "Apologies. Mairi has been away on maternity leave. She only got back last week and I want to take as much off her plate as possible. One of the things I was supposed to do, months ago as you say, was to hire an events organiser to sort out all this stuff. I'm not a fan of Christmas, to be honest, and I procrastinated and put it to the back of my mind until Mairi reminded me on Saturday."

"When you hunted me down in the Christmas shop."

"Yes. I had the idea that I could pop into the shop — I was between meetings — and could organise an order for some decorations for the house, but I got overwhelmed by the amount of stuff and then helped you retrieve your crown . . . and you seemed like the answer to my prayers . . ." A strange look passed across his face. He cleared his throat. "So to speak . . . Anyway, the gist of it is that I appreciate it's very late in the day and I haven't given you the easiest of tasks."

"I'll start calling around straight away and get back to you with what I manage to find . . ." Rose said.

"Great. The other thing I need help with is my own Christmas. As I said, I usually work a lot leading up to Christmas. Isla and I go to my sister's house in Manchester to celebrate so we never bother decorating, but my family has decided to descend upon us this year."

"You don't sound very happy about that," commented Rose. So, no wife presumably then if it was just Alastair and Isla going to his sister's for the holidays. What had happened to her?

"Like I said, I'm not a fan of Christmas in general, but my sister and her husband will be bringing their twins. My sister and I are close, and she always goes to a lot of trouble for Isla at Christmas, so it's important to me that they have a good time. And my aunt will be coming. Aunt Helena loves a traditional Christmas and she'll have plenty to say if she thinks I haven't gone to enough effort."

"Don't worry, I'm sure they'll all have a wonderful time."

"Basically, I need you to help buy and wrap presents for them and organise any activities you think the children would like to attend while they're here — Santa's Grotto, that kind of thing."

31

"I'll make a start organising venues and then I'll think about ideas for decorating the house and report back to you?"

"It's all in your hands," Alastair said. "I honestly have no idea about Christmas decorations and, frankly, I don't want to. If you speak to Mairi, she'll let you know the budget. You have free rein on my house for the festive period."

"You trust me to decorate your house however I want for Christmas?"

"Implicitly. Are you happy to use the library as your base?"

"Sure, I brought my laptop with me."

"Brilliant. Put your mobile number into my phone and I'll message you the Wi-Fi code — sorry, I should have thought to have done that last night." He handed her his iPhone.

She put her number in and handed it back, and he messaged her.

"There you go. I'll be in my office upstairs this morning if you need anything, but I'm sure whatever you decide will be great. Oh, and you're welcome to use either of the Land Rovers whenever you like. I've insured you on both."

Alastair and Rose both went rather awkwardly up the stairs together, her to retrieve her laptop from her room and he to his office which was the room next to his bedroom, she discovered. She walked behind him on the stairs, doing her best not to check out his perfectly curved bottom. *Behave*, she told herself firmly. *He's your boss and not to mention he must be so much older than you! He has a twelve-year-old daughter! He didn't look much above early thirties though . . .*

She shook her head to rid her mind of such ridiculous thoughts. They reached the top of the stairs and went their separate ways. Rose found herself giving a little wave to Alastair as he went into his office and flushed once again. Why had she done that? Would her face ever be its normal colour around this man?

* * *

Rose set her laptop up in the library and logged into the Wi-Fi without any problems. It was, without a doubt, the most beautiful space she'd ever worked in and the smell of old books and furniture polish was very comforting. The first job she completed was to email Mairi to touch base and get an idea of how much money she had to play with. She was beginning to google local venues when her phone rang.

"Hello," she said, answering it.

"Hi, Rose, it's Mairi. I thought it would be easier to call you rather than put everything in an email. I have sent you the budget though. Divide it up as you like. It's very generous and there's an accompanying credit card set up for you. Anyway, how was your journey? What impression did Edinburgh make on you in the five minutes you were there?" Mairi laughed.

"It seemed lovely. I hope I have a chance to look around it while I'm here."

"I would offer to show you around but, I'm not sure if Alastair told you, I had a baby a few months ago, and a whole day out in the city is honestly not going to happen."

"He did tell me, congratulations!" Rose said.

"Thank you, that's very sweet. Rory's wonderful, but definitely a handful and I'm still getting to grips with being back at work, even with me not being full-time now and with Alastair being absolutely brilliant."

"That's completely understandable."

"I still can't believe that he forgot to book an events organiser until now, mind you," Mairi said, with another laugh.

"I know, talk about last minute!"

"Do you think you'll be able to find venues?"

"I hope so," Rose said. What would happen if she couldn't book somewhere for Alastair to host his events? Would she find herself out of a job? Presumably there was a section in her contract that if she couldn't fulfil what was required of her then she'd be out on her ear and on a train back to London. Lucky she hadn't returned her Elsa costume . . .

* * *

Rose's stomach rumbled and she checked the time on her phone. It was almost 1 p.m. and she was no closer to finding a venue. Everything had been booked up months ago as she'd suspected, even the places that she really didn't think were right. She was scraping the bottom of the barrel now.

Mrs Reed had been very sweetly keeping her hydrated and caffeinated with regular cups of coffee and glasses of water, and she'd told Rose lunch was at one in the kitchen. So, when the time came, Rose got up and stretched her small frame, stiff after sitting for so long.

The smell of whatever Mrs Reed had been cooking hit Rose's nostrils as soon as she opened the library door onto the hallway and she followed it eagerly into the kitchen. Mrs Reed was slicing up a large round loaf of what looked like freshly baked sourdough.

"Hello, dear. Could you give the soup a stir for me, check it isn't catching?"

"Of course — it smells amazing."

"It's just leek and potato. Seems like the right sort of day for it."

Mrs Reed finished cutting the bread and set it out on a plate.

"Can I get the bowls?"

"Thank you, second cupboard along on your left."

Rose retrieved them and Mrs Reed began to serve up with a ladle.

"Would you mind running upstairs and letting Mr Duncan know his lunch is ready?"

"Of course, I'll be back in a minute." Rose ran up the stairs and knocked on Alastair's door.

"Come in!" he called and Rose popped her head round the door.

"Mrs Reed says it's time for lunch."

He stood up. "I'd better hurry then. It doesn't do to keep her waiting."

There was something rather sweet about this huge man of business, an actual laird, rushing to ensure he didn't make his housekeeper cross by letting the soup get cold.

They walked down the stairs together and back into the kitchen and sat down with Mrs Reed to eat.

"Any luck finding venues?" Alastair asked.

"Not yet, but I'm not completely out of options." Rose wasn't technically lying; there surely must be somewhere she hadn't tried yet. "This is really good soup, Mrs Reed," she added, hoping to change the course of the conversation.

"Thank you," said Mrs Reed.

There was a bang at the back door and Mrs Reid sighed.

"Houdini," Alastair explained. "He's not keen on the rain."

The goat knocked again and Mrs Reid got up and opened the back door a little. Houdini gave a happy bleat.

"You are a goat," Mrs Reid stated firmly. "And if you don't like getting wet, go in your shelter." She shook her head. "Wait there a minute."

She closed the door again and walked into the larder, returning with a large carrot in her hand. She reopened the door and gave it to the still-waiting goat.

"Off with you now," she said.

Houdini gave a happier bleat and walked off.

As if on cue, a mobile phone rang on the kitchen counter. Mrs Reed answered it. "Hello, Isla, is everything all right? Yes, I know it's raining. Yes, he's fine. I've just seen him. Yes, I'll check he has enough hay . . . I'll see you later." Mrs Reed ended the call with another sigh. "That child has us wrapped around her little finger."

Alastair shrugged. "You're the one feeding her goat carrots when he comes begging at the back door."

Mrs Reed humph-ed but didn't contradict him.

Alastair left for some business meetings in Edinburgh once he'd finished eating and Rose helped Mrs Reed to clean up, despite her protestations.

"This is a big house for you to be in charge of," Rose commented.

"We have some girls who come in to clean. And it's only Mr Duncan and Isla here now. It's not as if Mr Duncan entertains like his mother and father used to. They used to hold the most wonderful Christmas parties."

"Did they?" Rose tried to ignore her body's reaction to the confirmation that Alastair didn't have a wife.

"Absolutely, the house would look beautiful all lit up. And the guests were so glamorous . . ."

Rose froze, a plan suddenly appearing in her head. "Oh my goodness, thank you!" she said, surprising Mrs Reed with a hug. "You've just given me a wonderful idea."

CHAPTER 5

By the time Isla came home from school, Rose's plans were coming together nicely. It still hadn't been easy organising what she wanted at such late notice, but removing the need to find two venues out of the equation certainly made things easier.

Isla came straight to find her in the hope there was something she could do to help. "Not at the moment, but maybe in a little while," said Rose, smiling. She was still in the middle of making phone calls and sending emails. "Have you got homework to do?"

"A bit," admitted Isla.

"Want to set up next to me and get it out of the way?" asked Rose. "There's plenty of room. When you're done, you can help me go round the downstairs and work out what decorations I need to order."

"Okay," said Isla happily. She put her bag on the table and started taking out her books.

* * *

"You don't happen to know where Isla is, do you?" asked Mrs Reed, popping her head around the library door a couple of minutes later. "Oh, there you are!" she said, spotting the girl. "Would you like me to bring your snack in here?"

"Yes, please, Mrs Reed," said Isla.

A few minutes later, Mrs Reed reappeared with juice for Isla, decaf coffee for Rose and some homemade flapjacks before heading off home. The dogs, presumably lured by the smell of the flapjacks, settled down under the table.

At five o'clock, Alastair appeared at the library door.

"Any luck with the venues?" he asked coming into the room. "Isla, what are you doing here?" A strange look passed over his face as he took in the cosy scene.

"My homework," she replied.

"Are you telling me you're actually doing your homework without complaining about it for at least two hours beforehand?" asked Alastair, evidently incredulous.

"Yep! I started as soon as I got home from school. I'm almost done. Rose is very good at maths."

"Rose is trying to work."

"It's fine, really," said Rose, "I enjoy Isla's company. She's not disturbing me. The maths only took a couple of minutes."

"If you're sure," checked Alastair, uncertainly. "But, Isla, if Rose asks you to go, you do so without argument, okay?"

"Okay, Dad," Isla agreed, giving a little roll of her eyes.

Alastair left and Rose and Isla fell back into their respective tasks.

"I'm done," Isla announced fifteen minutes later.

"Great," Rose said, "because I think I am too. Do you still want to help me brainstorm how to decorate this big old house of yours?"

"Sure." Isla looked so excited.

The pair went into the hallway accompanied by the dogs. "I thought it would be great to have a huge Christmas tree in here so that it's the first thing people see when they come into the house," said Rose.

"That's a brilliant idea!" Isla grinned from ear to ear. "Can we get one so big that it almost touches the ceiling?"

"Sure . . ." Rose laughed. "But we need to decide what colour scheme we're going for and a theme. I was thinking of a winter wonderland, bringing lots of the outside inside. We could have white lights on the tree, warm ones not white-white, and lots more weaved in amongst greenery all around the downstairs."

"That sounds awesome! It's going to look so fancy with all the white and green!"

"That's the idea," said Rose laughing again at Isla's excitement.

They continued into the drawing room with its huge fireplace and mantel, planning what they could do. Numerous wingback chairs and side tables were dotted around and a grand piano sat invitingly in the corner. Next was the cosier sitting room full of comfy, battered sofas, a smaller fireplace and the only television. Family photos covered the walls of this room.

"We're going to need an awful lot of fairy lights," observed Rose.

"The more the better!" Isla declared.

"You're not still working, are you?" Alastair asked, coming into the room. "It's six and food's nearly ready."

"I just wanted to get some ideas from Isla before I began ordering decorations," Rose explained.

"Well, come through and eat now. Mrs Reed left us chicken stew and mashed potatoes."

"I think we're just about finished here if you agree, Isla?"

"I think so," Isla said with a nod.

"Why don't you take your school stuff up to your room, then, while I serve?" Alastair suggested.

"Okay, Dad." Isla headed back to the library.

"Do you mind eating with us again?" Alastair asked Rose once his daughter was out of earshot. "If you'd rather not, it's fine. You could take your dinner into the library or something."

"Thank you, but it would be lovely to eat with you." Rose tried not to smile at how solicitous her new boss was being.

She followed him into the kitchen where they served up the food Mrs Reed had prepared for them, and Isla joined them.

Isla filled them both in on her day at school while they ate. Houdini tried his luck once again at the back door and was rewarded with an apple from Isla.

Once they'd finished, Isla went upstairs to have a bath and Rose helped Alastair to tidy up.

"Dare I ask — any luck finding venues?" Alastair was loading the dishwasher.

"Kind of," Rose said, suddenly nervous about what she was about to suggest. "Mrs Reed gave me a really good idea earlier. She was talking about how your mum and dad used to throw the most amazing Christmas parties, so I had the idea that we could host the parties here . . ."

"Here?" repeated Alastair slowly, a frown forming as he rinsed a plate.

"Yes. We can hold the less formal party in the house. We just need to move some of the furniture around, and Mrs Reed says there are extra tables and chairs in the attic. There should be plenty of room for the number of people you want to invite. Plus, because it'll already be decorated, there won't be the cost to decorate a different venue. The more formal, black-tie party will also be held here, but in the garden. I've hired an enormous marquee and there'll be a sit-down dinner and dancing afterwards. The marquee company also supply heaters so there won't be any problems with people being cold."

"Rose, there's a reason I don't host Christmas parties in my home," Alastair said. "I'm a very private person and I don't want a load of drunk people here making a mess and damaging things. You're going to have to change it."

Rose's heart sank. She'd thought that Alastair would be pleased she'd managed to find a solution. It was fair to say that she hadn't considered that he hadn't continued his parents' traditions because he didn't *want* to.

"There isn't anywhere else," she explained, wiping down the now cleared table. "I spent hours calling anywhere and everywhere, but everything is booked up. And the formal event won't even be in the house, it'll be in the front garden.

You can escape and hide in your study after a while if you like, no one will know."

That elicited a small smile.

"Anyway," Rose continued, "how crazy do you imagine your employees will get?"

Alastair nodded. "You have a point, they're good people."

"And I imagine they'll be too worried about getting in trouble with their boss to do more than nibble a vol-au-vent before heading home early."

"Fine . . ." Alastair agreed, albeit with a reluctant sigh. Unease was still present in his eyes.

"Thank you! The events will go so smoothly and I'll have a cleaning crew come in first thing in the morning. The place will look better after the party than it did before."

"I'll hold you to that," Alastair said, shaking his head and drying his hands on a tea towel.

Technically he was agreeing, but Rose knew he still wasn't happy and she felt bad as they went through dates and she got his agreement to the ones she suggested. If there were any other option, she'd be turning to it, but there wasn't. She'd just have to make sure she made things as pain-free for Alastair as possible.

CHAPTER 6

Rose was back at her laptop at nine the next morning, putting in orders for decorations and making shopping lists for things she'd need to pick up herself. She reserved three Christmas trees to be delivered, one for the hallway and two to go either side of the front door. She also booked a company to put lights on the outside of the house, who happened to be free to come in just a couple of hours. Luck seemed to be on her side.

Next, now that she knew the dates and venue, she needed to get onto the invitations. All the invites for the people who worked for Alastair would be sent out via email but she designed and ordered printed invitations to the more formal event to be sent out as soon as possible.

She took a break from working on them when the Christmas lights people arrived and she went out to greet them and check they understood what she wanted done — white lights around the front of the house and surrounding the door and windows.

She hadn't seen Alastair all day; Mrs Reed had even taken his lunch up to him, but he put his head around the library door just after 2 p.m.

"Hey, just wanting to check you have everything you need?" he said.

"I think I'm good, thank you," Rose replied.

"Did you receive the list of the people I thought we should invite to the second event?" He came into the room, and sat down on the opposite side of the table. The bizarre thought came into Rose's mind that she could probably reach him with her foot if she really stretched . . . She shook her head and inwardly scolded herself.

"I did and Mairi sent me over a few more."

"Great. Oh, by the way, you're very welcome to invite someone . . . a boyfriend or . . . girlfriend . . . I mean, you could be married . . . Anyway, book an extra place if you have someone you'd like to invite."

Rose fought back a smile at his awkwardness. "I'm not married and I don't have a boyfriend or girlfriend or anyone I'd like to invite. But thank you for the offer . . ."

"If you're sure . . ."

"I am," Rose replied, feeling her cheeks reddening. "Will you . . . um, be bringing anyone?"

"No," came the firm response. So, he was presumably single then, Rose noted. She chose to ignore what this knowledge did to her stomach.

"Have you got a few minutes to chat through the plans for when your family come to stay?" she asked, bringing her mind back to business.

"Absolutely."

"Great," replied Rose. "So, it's your sister, her husband, their twin six-year-old sons and your aunt who are coming?" She'd come to the conclusion that Isla's mother, whoever she was, didn't live with Alastair or really seem to be present in Isla's life at all from what she could tell, but it seemed rude to ask directly whether she'd be joining them for Christmas or whether Isla would be spending at least part of her school holidays with her mother . . . Maybe she'd died, Rose realised with horror. She quickly rearranged her face to stop it from betraying her thoughts.

"That's right," confirmed Alastair.

"And there aren't any other . . . arrangements that I need to know about?" Rose asked carefully.

Alastair gave her an odd look. "Not that I can think of."

Rose quickly continued, "I was also wondering if you have any traditions I should be aware of, stuff that I need to make sure I book in . . . I have some ideas but I don't want to miss anything out."

"Oh, um, not really. We usually head to my sister's house in Manchester on Christmas Eve and come back on the twenty-seventh. So, just regular Christmas eating and playing games. Isla loves to watch Christmas movies with her cousins. Oh, my sister usually insists upon playing charades after Christmas lunch — which is always turkey, but we'll probably get a takeaway this year as Mrs Reed won't be here over Christmas and I would most likely burn the house down if I tried to cook Christmas lunch."

Rose refrained from commenting about how terrible it sounded to have a takeaway on Christmas Day.

"A couple of times, Fiona has booked tickets to the pantomime . . . Aunt Helena will flat-out refuse to come to that, but the kids will enjoy it. I think that's everything."

"Okay, thanks," said Rose. "I'll come back to you with some ideas."

"I'm sure whatever you decide will be great," Alastair said. "As you may have gathered, I'm not great at this Christmas stuff . . ."

"That's why you hired me." Rose gave a little salute. "Let me show you the proposed menu for the second event . . ."

Her mobile rang. "Oh, sorry," she mouthed to Alastair as she answered. "Hello? . . . Yes, this is Rose . . . Oh . . . Yes, I completely understand, I just really wanted them here sooner . . . Can I give you a call back?"

She ended the conversation with a sigh.

"That was the farm I ordered the Christmas trees from. They were supposed to be bringing them this evening, but the guy who does the deliveries has hurt his back and now they don't know when they're going to be able to make it. I wanted to be able to decorate them tomorrow."

"How far away are they?"

"It's about a fifteen minute drive I think . . ."

"Phone them and tell them we're on our way. Between the two of us, we can get them strapped onto the back of my Land Rover. I'm not even going to ask why exactly I need multiple trees . . ."

"Trust me, you do and they'll look really good, but are you sure you have time?"

"Sure. I've been sat behind a desk all day so far, it'll do me good to stretch my legs."

Five minutes later, Rose had called to confirm they could go and pick up the trees themselves and had put on her coat and scarf. Alastair was waiting for her by the front door with Houdini.

"Apparently the goat is coming with us," Alastair explained. "He'll drive Mrs Reed crazy if we leave him here."

"Is he safe in the car?" Rose asked.

"Yeah, he has a crate in the back for when I take Isla to school."

"Okay then, I guess we're taking a goat Christmas tree shopping!"

Alastair secured the goat in his crate, getting some very strange looks from the people putting up the lights, and they got into Alastair's car.

The drive didn't take long and Alistair pointed out local landmarks along the way.

"Are you sure you don't mind being dragged away from work to do this? You know I probably could have managed by myself . . ." Rose said.

Alastair gave a little laugh. "It's fine, I needed a break anyway. Plus, you're like five foot nothing — I think it's probably for the best that I'm there as well."

"You make a fair point," she admitted, as they turned off the main road and down a lane with signs leading to the Christmas tree farm.

"This place looks really nice," commented Alastair.

"I'm guessing you haven't been here before?"

"No, we never usually bother with a Christmas tree."

"Oh, right," Rose said quietly. Who didn't get at least a little Christmas tree for their kid?

They pulled up outside the cabin serving as the Christmas tree farm's office and Alastair told Houdini in no uncertain terms that he was staying in the car. The goat bleated grumpily but appeared to accept his fate, turning round and lying down with a sigh.

Alastair and Rose got out of the car and were greeted by a boy in his late teens.

Rose explained who they were.

"Really sorry for the inconvenience," the boy said. "You can take your pick from the pre-cut ones over there, or you can chop down your own from the paddock on the right," he instructed.

Alastair looked at Rose. "Why do I get the feeling you're going to want to cut these trees ourselves?"

"Honestly, it's going to be mainly you doing the cutting, but yeah . . ." Rose admitted. "I've never done that before and it seems a shame to miss the opportunity."

"Fine," said Alastair, with a little snort.

They accepted the offered gardening gloves and hacksaw, and walked over to the Christmas tree paddock. It being midweek and still only early December, there wasn't anyone else visiting the farm.

"We need one fairly big one," Rose said, wandering between the trees, "And then a couple of smaller ones . . ."

"What have I let myself in for?" she heard Alastair mutter to himself.

"A magical Christmas," Rose retorted with a grin.

"How exactly are we going to fit all these on the Land Rover?"

"That thing is massive and the trees will be netted up . . . One of the little ones at least could go inside if we put the seats down . . ."

"Okay, that would probably work," Alastair admitted.

Finding the larger tree was easy and only took Rose a few moments.

"Are you sure you're happy with this one? It's huge," commented Alastair.

"That's a good thing. You have a very high ceiling in that entrance hall of yours. Unless you'd rather get a smaller one?"

"I trust your judgment completely," Alastair said solemnly.

"This is the one then."

Alastair bent down and began sawing the tree. Rose looked away once she realised she was staring. She wondered how large his arm muscles were . . .

They lugged the first tree back to the car with Rose carrying the top end and Alastair insisting on taking most of the weight.

Once the tree was netted by the boy and on the roof of the car, they returned to the paddock to pick out the other two trees. It proved a harder job. Rose wanted them to be the same height and shape, so they could frame the front door.

"Do you think anywhere will deliver breakfast to us here if you still haven't chosen by morning?" Alastair commented after twenty minutes.

"Don't you want your house to look perfect for Christmas?" Rose asked.

"I'm looking forward to when Christmas is over and my home gets back to normal," admitted Alastair.

Rose gave an understanding smile. "Truth be told, I'm not the biggest fan of Christmas anymore either," she admitted. "I mean, I'm not a total Scrooge or anything, I think it's nice for kids, but I'll also be glad when it's over and regular life resumes."

But would she, Rose wondered. Yes, she wasn't looking forward to Christmas itself, but she was enjoying her work and organising Christmas for someone else, and once Christmas was here, she'd be back in London trying to work out what on earth to do with her life.

"It must be strange organising celebrations for other people and not doing so for yourself," Alastair replied.

"Honestly, I wasn't planning to do anything for Christmas this year. The only effect that Christmas was going to have on me was that my job in the shop would come to an end."

"And you'd have to return your crown and dress?"

"Exactly. I'm sure you can imagine the wrench that was going to be." Rose said dryly. "Okay, this tree, and the one we saw in the corner over there," she declared.

"You are quite sure?"

"Positive. Let's get them chopped down and head back. It's freezing out here."

* * *

Rose and Alastair arrived back at the house with the trees still all intact to find the outside lights were still being put up. Rose stopped to talk with the workmen while Alastair took the trees off the car and then went inside. Rose got the impression that he had stuff to catch up on.

Once she'd checked the workmen were happy and offered them more hot drinks only to discover Mrs Reed had, of course, already made them some already, Rose returned to the library to continue with work.

* * *

Isla came home from school while Rose was in the middle of sending out the email invitations to Alastair's staff. She'd wanted to personalise them, so it was taking a while.

"Are those Christmas trees outside?" Isla asked, marching straight into the library.

"Yes, they are. The farm couldn't deliver them so your dad and I went to get them this afternoon."

"I can't believe you didn't wait for me to come and get the Christmas trees!" Isla wailed.

"I'm sorry, we couldn't. The Christmas tree farm only stays open until it gets dark so by the time you were home it would have been too late."

"You could have picked me up early from school!" suggested Isla. Rose gave her a look which conveyed exactly what she thought of that idea.

"I'll save the big tree to decorate with you tomorrow after school, how about that?"

"Okay," conceded Isla. "As long as I get to put the star on the top."

"It's a deal."

Isla once again settled down next to Rose to get her homework done.

* * *

Alastair came in to say hello to his daughter a little later.

"Isla, you have a perfectly good desk in your room."

"She's no trouble," said Rose.

"I like being down here. And you should be happy I'm finally doing my homework straight after school like you've been wanting me to for years," retorted Isla.

"Okay, fine." Alastair threw his hands in the air. "But you should stop working, Rose. You finished late last night."

"I'll finish up soon, I just want to get all these emails out."

"Okay," said Alastair. "Thanks for all your hard work."

"And thank you for helping me pick up the Christmas trees. They're going to look great."

"I'll take your word for that," said Alastair with a smile.

"Have you got a minute to show Isla what's been put up today?" Rose asked. She noticed Isla's eyes light up with curiosity.

"Sure." Alastair smiled.

They trooped outside, followed by the dogs, and stood in front of the house. Rose showed Isla where the switch was and the child gasped as she pushed it and turned on the lights covering the building.

"Oh, wow!" said Isla. "It looks gorgeous."

Rose had to agree. The lights illuminated the grey granite house, making it seem homely and welcoming.

"What do you think?" she asked Alastair.

"Very festive," he answered with a shrug.

"Oh, come on, Dad! Don't be so grouchy!" chided Isla.

Alastair laughed. "It does look good. Thanks for organising it, Rose."

"It was my pleasure," Rose said as Isla pulled her into a hug.

* * *

Isla was practically jumping up and down with excitement the following afternoon when she got home to find the trees finally ready to decorate.

"They look so good!" she exclaimed. "The one in the hall is *huge*! Can we start on them now?"

"Don't you think you should get your homework done first?"

"I've only got a little bit left because I did some at lunchtime. I can finish it after dinner."

"If that's all right with your dad, then we can do it now," Rose said.

Isla went running upstairs to check with Alastair. A moment later she returned, gleeful that he'd agreed.

"Are those all the decorations?" Isla asked, pointing to the piles of bags and boxes in the corner of the library.

"Yep. I was shopping for them for hours today! But it's just the two big boxes on the end that have the decorations for the tree in. They're not heavy so why don't you take them out to the hallway? The lights are already on — your lovely gardener, Mac did them earlier. I'll be there as soon as I've sent this email."

* * *

"Wow!" said Isla, stepping back to look at the completed tree. "It looks so posh!"

The all-white theme worked well and contrasted beautifully with the dark green pine needles. White baubles with silver glitter adorned the branches and a silver star graced the top of the tree.

"It does, doesn't it?" agreed Rose. "We did a good job."

"I want Dad to see it," Isla declared and she raced upstairs, returning a moment later with her father following behind. He didn't look overly impressed to be dragged away from his office, Rose noticed.

"Isn't it huge, Dad?" Isla said.

"It's certainly that," Alastair commented.

"Oh, come on, it looks good!" coaxed Rose.

"It does," admitted Alastair. "Now, may I get back to work, please?"

Isla laughed. "Okay!"

Rose began clearing up the discarded packaging. She'd keep some of it to store the decorations in for next year. When she most likely wouldn't be here to decorate the tree. She'd have a different job by then and wouldn't be able to take almost a month off to come to Scotland even if Alastair invited her back.

"The lights are all set up on the trees outside as well," Rose said, while scolding herself for being ridiculous. "Would you like to have the honour of turning them on? They're going to be set to work via a timer but I thought you might like to do the first turn on."

"Of course, I would!" cried Isla. "I'll get Houdini."

They grabbed their coats and Houdini and the dogs joined them for a solemn ceremony of the official switching on of the Christmas tree lights.

"Thank you so much, Rose," said Isla, hugging her with one hand, the other keeping a tight grip on Houdini. "It's going to be so great to have the house looking all Christmassy and to be spending Christmas at home. I like going to Auntie Fiona's, but it'll be fun to have everyone here."

"I bet it will," said Rose. "Now let's go back in the warm and you can get that homework done while I finish tidying up."

"At least I get out of the tidying up, I suppose," Isla mock-grumbled as she headed back indoors, followed by the animals.

Rose was so glad that Isla liked what she was doing to get everything ready for Christmas, but it was a big responsibility and she already worried she'd messed up by not being able to bring Isla along to choose the Christmas trees. She'd have to do something to remedy that. Isla was so excited about having Christmas at home for the first time in her life — what if Rose messed it up? What if Isla had some idea of how she wanted Christmas to go and Rose was getting it all wrong? She seemed happy with what was happening so far, but Rose decided she'd have to make sure she really listened to Isla so that she picked up on any hints she dropped. Because the house was being used as a backdrop for a work event, she felt it did need to look a certain way and not like Christmas just exploded all over it, but she could definitely add in some aspects especially for Isla once the first event was over.

CHAPTER 7

Rose spent the next couple of days decorating the ground floor of the house — with Isla's help whenever she was available — and organising the two Christmas events. The first, the employees' event, was scheduled for the following Friday. The caterers were confirmed, thanks to Mairi who had been able to call in a favour. It seemed luck was on Rose's side.

Unfortunately, she hadn't had any such joy with finding a DJ for that event, but she'd put together a playlist and hired a karaoke machine which she hoped would be fun and that everyone would enjoy. She wasn't sure quite how Alastair would react to that particular news though so was waiting for the right moment to tell him. She suspected that moment might not come before the party itself.

The Friday before the first event, Rose finished work for the day and was sketching in her room — something she now did whenever she had some down time. Her phone dinged with a message from Alastair: *Could you check on dinner? I'll be down as soon as I can. I'm just trying to finish something.*

No problem, Rose messaged back. In the kitchen, a delicious-smelling lasagne was in the oven. It looked done so she turned the oven off and took the salad Mrs Reed had made out of the fridge.

With Isla's help, she laid the table and mixed up a salad dressing before Alastair made an appearance.

"Thanks for this," he said, distractedly pouring himself a glass of water. He seemed preoccupied as he bent down to scratch a dog behind the ears.

"Is everything all right?" Rose asked, lifting the lasagne out of the oven and popping it on the table mat.

Noticing the food, Alastair took the oven gloves from Rose. "Sorry, you shouldn't be doing that. You sit down, let me serve up."

Rose took a seat and accepted the plate of food Alastair handed her before he served his daughter.

"So, it looks like I need to travel down to London tomorrow," he explained as he dished up a portion for himself. "There's a business thing I have to attend, but Mrs Reed has her sons visiting so I don't have anyone to watch Isla." He turned to his daughter and said, "How do you fancy a trip to London this weekend?"

"I've got a hockey match tomorrow afternoon, and Lucy's birthday cinema trip on Sunday, remember?" Isla's eyes were filled with panic. "I don't want to sit on a train for hours and then wait around while you're in your meeting."

"I'm sorry, sweetheart, but I really do have to go to London early tomorrow morning. We could go to Wagamama in the evening and—"

"Or Rose could look after me," interrupted Isla, giving Rose a hopeful smile.

"Isla, Rose has got her own things to do . . ."

"Of course I will," Rose said quickly, seeing Isla's smile beginning to fade. "I was just going to suggest it."

"I can't ask you to do that," Alastair declared.

"You don't have to. I'm offering."

Alastair opened his mouth to protest again, but Rose cut him off. "Honestly, it's fine. I don't have any plans for the weekend. I'd love to hang out with Isla. If you leave me the car, I'll take her to hockey and the cinema . . ."

54

"And to Claire's Accessories after my match tomorrow so I can get Lucy a present . . ."

"Isla . . ." warned Alastair.

Rose laughed. "Of course we can."

"Rose, this is very kind of you but we couldn't possibly take advantage of you like that."

"You wouldn't be taking advantage. We'll have a great time."

"Can I at least offer to pay you for your time?" Alastair said.

"Thank you for the offer, but no." As handy as the money would be, she didn't like the idea of Isla feeling that Rose needed to be paid to spend time with her. And she genuinely would enjoy being with her. What else would she do with herself in this huge house if both Alastair and Isla went to London? Drawing, of course, but she'd still be able to do that and look after Isla.

"This is going to be the best weekend ever!" cried Isla.

"So you're not going to miss me at all?" Alastair shook his head but was laughing all the same.

"Not really, Dad. It's only one night, isn't it?"

"Yes," reassured Alastair. "I'll be home for dinner on Sunday."

"Great," confirmed Isla.

They finished eating and Isla left to shower and to do some homework.

"I can clean up, you go and relax," Alastair said to Rose as he got up from the table.

"I'm happy to help. You look tired," said Rose. He really did. His hair was more messed up than usual and he had bags under his eyes.

Alastair smiled. "Yeah, things have been a bit busy," he admitted. "I was looking forward to hanging out with Isla this weekend but then this turned up . . ."

"We'll have a brilliant time and she'll get to go to everything she's been looking forward to."

"I'd better go and book my train tickets and a cab to pick me up in the morning as Mairi's clocked off for the day." Alastair stifled a yawn.

"Depending on the train time on Sunday, I could maybe come and pick you up from the station?" Rose offered. She knew she was being silly and that he was perfectly capable of looking after himself and certainly didn't need her fussing over him, but he looked so tired and she wanted to do something to help him.

"Thanks, but don't worry. I can just take a cab. It's a long drive and I think Isla's birthday thing is in the opposite direction."

"Okay, well, you've got my number if you're stuck."

"I appreciate that and thank you again for looking after Isla. I'll need to leave early tomorrow, so I'll see you Sunday. I'll message to let you know what time I'll be back."

"See you then," said Rose.

* * *

Rose heard the taxi arrive for Alastair at 5 a.m. and was grateful it wasn't her having to get up so early. When she did heave herself out of bed at eight, Isla's bedroom door was still closed so she crept past as quietly as she could to use the bathroom, hoping the outdated system would agree to let her have some hot water that morning. She was in luck, a sure sign that it was going to be a good day.

By the time she was dressed, Isla's door was open and she found her ward in the kitchen getting breakfast.

"I'm not sure Mrs Reed would approve of you having Coco Pops for breakfast," Rose said, coming into the room and stepping over a sleeping dog. She spotted an envelope with her name on it on the table.

Isla giggled. "Dad lets me have them at the weekend. Mrs Reed keeps trying to hide them at the back of the pantry, but I always manage to find them. Would you like a bowl?"

"Why not?" said Rose. "I haven't had them for years."

She opened the envelope and found some cash and a note from Alastair saying to get a takeaway for herself and Isla that evening.

"Your dad's left us some money to get a treat for dinner tonight."

"Can we get pizza?"

"That sounds like a really good idea. Will they deliver out here?"

"We have to collect it, I'm afraid."

"That's no problem," Rose said.

Isla poured Rose a large bowl of cereal and passed it to her. "Don't worry, I'm going to have some toast and peanut butter as well."

"That's probably a good idea, especially with your match this afternoon."

Apparently, Houdini also had to have some toast fed to him by the back door which he seemed to enjoy.

"I was thinking of going for a walk after breakfast, would you like to come?" Rose asked Isla as they cleared up.

"Sure! I can show you around and we can climb my favourite hill."

Rose hadn't actually planned on hill climbing being involved in her intended stroll along the lane leading away from the house, but Isla looked so excited.

"That sounds great," Rose said, as convincingly as she could.

"Houdini and the dogs will need to come as well. They'll be sad if we leave them at home."

"Okay." This outing was getting more and more complicated by the second.

"Have you got walking boots or wellies? It's going to be super muddy."

"I haven't, I'm afraid," said Rose, part of her hoping that would get her out of going on what could surely officially now be called a hike. A thought that frankly terrified her.

"Don't worry, what size feet are you?"

"Four?"

"I'm a five, but I have some older wellies that are a four. I'll go and get them."

Isla ran upstairs happily to retrieve the boots while Rose wondered what on earth she had let herself in for.

* * *

They set off along the lane, half an hour later, the dogs and Houdini on leads, but Isla soon led them over a stile into a field which had a little side entrance for the dogs and Houdini.

"Are you sure it's okay for us to be going through here?" Rose asked, anxiously. She didn't want an angry farmer turning up waving a shotgun and yelling at them to get off his land.

"Oh yeah, Dad doesn't mind. We just need to stick to the edges if there are any animals in here."

"Your dad owns all this?"

"Yeah," replied Isla with a shrug. "The estate's pretty big."

Rose was aware of the size of Alastair's property from her research while in London, but reading some figures on a computer screen and actually looking out over how vast it was, were two very different things.

They continued walking through fields, some of them containing goats which Houdini ignored, his nose stuck in the air.

It began to drizzle, but Rose seemed the only one of the party even vaguely bothered by it. Isla just put her hood up and the animals didn't seem to notice.

They soon lost sight of the house which Rose had been using as something of a compass point. She wasn't used to walking in the countryside. Her landmarks when walking in London were structures and buildings and she could always just check Google Maps on her phone if she wasn't completely sure of her location. Actually, she thought, maybe that would still work here . . .

She took her phone out of her pocket surreptitiously so she could just get an idea of where they were in relation to the house, and, most importantly, how they were going to get back. But her phone had absolutely no signal. She stared at it in vague bewilderment, had she ever seen it with not a single bar of signal before?

No one even knew that they were out there . . . She really should have texted someone to tell them that they were heading out into the middle of nowhere with no survival gear or emergency food rations — not even a map for goodness' sake! And she was supposed to be in charge! Isla was completely her responsibility at the moment.

Okay, she was maybe overreacting, she told herself sternly. They'd only been walking for about twenty minutes according to her watch, though it certainly felt much longer. They could just retrace their steps if necessary.

Isla seemed very confident of her destination, but Rose felt she had to ask, "You do know where we're going, don't you?"

Isla laughed. "Of course, I do. I've been coming up here with my dad since I was about three years old!"

Rose felt a little reassured, but she really couldn't tell how Isla could be so nonchalant; all these fields looked very similar. Except they were getting steeper now and her thighs were beginning to ache. Why didn't she stick with that spin class she went to twice?

"This is the hill I was telling you about!" said Isla excitedly. "There used to be a fort on the top because of how high up it is. It gives you a really great view. Dad told me all about the history of it. I can't remember much though. There was a big fire hundreds of years ago or something which destroyed it but you can still see some of the markings on the ground."

They continued climbing. Rose could understand why marauders might think twice before invading here; they'd definitely need to have built up their cardio before attempting it. Though Isla didn't seem to be at all out of breath.

"The fort had more than one wall around it," explained Isla. "This is where the first one was."

Rose looked at where Isla was pointing, but couldn't make out anything that would show you there had been any sort of wall there.

"Here we are!" Isla cried as the hill finally began to level off. *How high did a hill have to be before it was technically a mountain?*

"Race you to the trig point!" Isla shouted and she and the animals careered off into the distance.

What on earth is a trig point? Rose wailed internally as she set off after them at a pained jog. She caught up with the group at a concrete triangular pillar set at the top of the hill. The pillar's top was broad and flat enough for Isla to use it as a seat, with Houdini doing his best to join her. The dogs ran back to Rose when they saw her and she petted their heads.

She took a moment to look around. She wasn't sure the view was completely worth the climb, but she had to admit it was pretty spectacular. The rugged landscape with its bare trees and farm animals dotted around was stark but beautiful. And she could see the house again. It wasn't all that far away, she had to admit.

"Have you got your phone with you?" Isla asked. "Can we take a selfie and send it to Dad when we get back home?"

"Of course we can," said Rose. "If you hop down we can get all the animals in it as well."

Isla climbed down off the pillar and she and Rose knelt with the animals and took some selfies with the humans pulling a variety of silly faces and the animals appearing rather perplexed.

* * *

The walk back was easier than the walk up, and Rose was feeling much happier now that she had her bearings. It also helped that the rain had paused. She was cold though and was very pleased when they reached the house.

Isla went through the selfies they'd taken and chose a couple for Rose to send to her dad then went up to her room to do some more of her homework before lunch. It still felt a little strange to be alone downstairs in Alastair's house but not as much as she'd have thought it would. It was a welcoming space and she felt comfortable there. She made herself a coffee and settled down in a large squishy armchair in the sitting room with her sketch-pad and pencil. It seemed like the perfect activity as the rain restarted and grew steadily stronger against the windows.

Rose became lost in her drawing and didn't hear Isla coming up behind her.

"Hi, Rose," she said, making Rose jump. "What are you drawing? Is that our house? It's really good!"

"Yes, or an attempt at it," said Rose, closing her sketch-book. "How did your homework go?"

"Good, I'm all finished, and I'm starving."

"Let's get some lunch then." Rose, checked the time. "We've got an hour before we need to leave for your hockey game."

"Can we make cheese toasties?"

"Good idea. I spotted the toasted sandwich maker in a cupboard the other day."

"We better make sure that we clean it properly afterwards," warned Isla. "Dad didn't once and Mrs Reed was so cross with him."

Rose laughed. "I'll make sure we don't get into trouble."

* * *

The pair had lunch then Rose tidied up while Isla got her stuff together for her match.

"You all ready to go?" asked Rose when she came back downstairs in her hockey kit.

"I think so. I'm feeling a bit nervous."

Rose went over and hugged Isla. "Just try your best and work with your teammates. That's all you can do. I'll be cheering you on from the sidelines."

Isla gave a little smile. "Could you take some photos for Dad?"

"Not a problem."

"He usually tries to come to all my matches."

"Hopefully he can be at the next one."

"I hope you don't get rained on too much."

"Me too." Rose laughed. "But I'll be bringing an umbrella so I should stay fairly dry. Have you got everything you need? Should you take water and a snack?"

"They provide that for us there. You fuss just like Dad!"

"Sorry!" apologised Rose.

"It's okay, I like it," said Isla with a shrug.

Rose steeled herself before saying, "Houdini's going to have to stay at home today," as firmly as she could.

"But he'll want to come to see me play!" whined Isla.

"Sweetheart, he's had lots of fun this morning, but I cannot manage to watch you play as well as taking care of a goat. And I thought you wanted to go to Claire's Accessories afterwards? Are you telling me they let goats in?"

"He can stay in the car," suggested Isla.

"He'll be so bored for such a long time. He'll be much happier at home."

Isla didn't look convinced.

"He can be warm and cosy in his shelter with lots of hay and we'll make a big fuss of him when we get back."

"Okay . . . you're probably right," Isla murmured. "I'll just go and check on him quickly and say bye."

"Great." That had actually been easier than Rose had anticipated.

Rose and Isla got in the Land Rover and Rose put the heating on and programmed the satnav to lead them to the school Isla's match was being held at.

"Can we listen to some music?" Isla asked.

"Sure." Isla soon had K-pop blasting out of the speakers.

* * *

Isla ran off to find her coach and teammates as soon as they'd parked up so Rose took her time making her way to the pitch. She wished she could watch the match from the comfort of the toasty warm car but she wasn't sure which part of the playing field Isla's match would be on. At least the rain had calmed down now.

She pulled her gloves and hat on and wound a big blue scarf around her neck. She walked over to where a group of parents, mainly mums it looked like, were gathered. Presumably, they knew the best place to stand for a decent view.

The girls were warming up on the pitch. It was easy to spot Isla as she was one of the tallest.

"Hi, who are you with? I don't think I've seen you here before," asked a woman with perfect hair and make-up.

"Isla," said Rose. "I haven't been to watch her before."

"Oh, hi! I'm Sarah, Lucy's mum. Isla's coming to my daughter's birthday trip tomorrow."

"I'm Rose. Nice to meet you. I'll be dropping Isla off tomorrow as well."

"Alastair not around this weekend then?"

Rose felt the attention of every other woman in the group fall on her as she said, "No, he's away on business."

"Oh," Sarah said, "What a shame! He's such a great dad. He's always here watching her matches!"

"Yeah, he's disappointed but Isla asked me to take some photos to send to him."

"So you're Isla's new nanny . . . ?" asked another woman.

"No, I'm just helping Alastair out this weekend." Glances were exchanged between the women.

"I'm sure he's very grateful," said Sarah. "It must be so hard for him bringing up Isla all by himself. We all offer to help but he's so self-sufficient . . ."

It looked like Isla's mother, whoever she was, wasn't in the picture at all, Rose reflected . . .

"I'm sure he'd ask if he needed anything." *Blimey*, Rose thought to herself, absorbing how popular Alastair seemed to be. Not that she could blame the mums, she supposed. She didn't think she'd ever known anyone as good-looking as Alastair in real life. She wondered if any of these women had dated him . . .

A whistle blew and everyone's focus moved to the pitch where the game had just started. Rose felt butterflies in her stomach as she manoeuvred herself to the side of the group so she could see properly and could get a clear shot for a half-decent photo to send to Alastair.

* * *

It wasn't that Rose wasn't enjoying watching Isla play, she was, although it was nerve-wracking, but it was so cold that by the time the whistle blew for half-time, she could no longer feel her feet.

"There's a coffee place just around the corner if you need a warm drink," said Sarah as everyone started to move around. "They usually do twenty minutes for half-time so the kids can have a break and use the loo if they need to."

"Thanks," said Rose gratefully. She looked over to see if she could spot Isla over at the refreshments and managed to catch her eye. Isla waved back happily and Rose signalled that she was going to get a drink. Isla gave her a thumbs up back.

* * *

Soon after the second half started, the opposing team pulled into the lead. Rose had to be careful how hard she squeezed her coffee cup as she watched anxiously. She knew Isla would be so disappointed if her team lost. Then Isla's team equalised and Rose could begin to breathe normally again, but her eyes were still locked on the game. Isla glanced over at her every now and again and Rose waved back each time.

There was only five minutes left in the match when Isla scored. Rose cheered with excitement, so happy that she'd started recording just a few seconds before and had managed to catch it on video for Alastair. Her heart was in her mouth for the last few minutes before the final whistle blew and Isla and her teammates cheered in celebration.

Rose went over to congratulate Isla and her friends before telling her to take as long as she needed getting changed and chatting. Then she headed back to the car to defrost and get away from all the women desperate to find out more about Alastair.

The car warmed up quickly with the heating cranked up to high and Rose took her gloves off and scrolled through the photos and videos she'd taken to choose the best ones to send to Alastair. She deleted any that were no good. Some of the photos taken at the top of the hill were really cute, especially one where Houdini was sticking his tongue out at the camera. She messaged Alastair four photos and the video of Isla scoring her goal.

Isla came over to the car with a huge smile on her face.

"Congratulations! You were amazing!" Rose said as Isla opened the passenger door.

"Thank you! I can't believe it!"

"I managed to catch your goal on camera and I sent it to your dad."

"Thank you!"

"Are you ready to go to Claire's?"

"Yes! Can we also go to TK Maxx if we have time? I wanted to get Dad some coffee and biscuits from there for Christmas."

"Great plan. And how about we stop off at Starbucks for a treat?"

"Excellent!"

* * *

It was dark when Rose and Isla returned home but the Christmas lights had turned on automatically, making the house look welcoming, and Rose smiled.

"Wow," she said, looking up at the sky. "You can see so many stars here."

"Yeah, Dad says it's because there isn't a lot of light pollution around here," said Isla.

Isla went upstairs to shower, but only after visiting Houdini in his enclosure to give him his dinner and tell him now much she'd missed him. Rose breathed a sigh of relief that the goat had stayed inside the enclosure while they were out. She'd half expected to be wandering the countryside looking for him all night.

Rose made herself a cup of tea and kept half an eye on the goat through the window while she unpacked the bags from their little shopping trip. Isla had been really pleased with the hair accessories she'd picked out for her friend and the presents for Alastair. She'd taken ages to choose the perfect card and gift bag in the card shop, but Rose hadn't minded. And they'd had a great time in Starbucks together chatting about Christmas which reassured Rose that she was on the right track with what she was planning. It was lovely to hear how excited Isla was.

Alastair had called to speak to Isla and she'd sounded so proud when she took him through the game blow by blow. "Rose, what time can we order the food?" asked Isla as she came into the kitchen.

"Soon if you like, just let me have my tea."

"Domino's isn't too far away. . ." said Isla hopefully.

"That's perfect then." Rose pulled the Domino's menu up on her phone. "Do you know what you'd like?"

"Pepsi, garlic bread and a pepperoni pizza, please. And can we get Ben & Jerry's? To celebrate my winning goal?"

"I think that's fair." Rose laughed. "Does your dad let you have Pepsi?"

"For special occasions," said Isla. "I think this counts."

"I agree."

"What's your favourite Ben & Jerry's ice cream flavour?"

"It's Chunky Monkey, but you can never get it anywhere," lamented Rose.

"Chunky Monkey?"

"See, you've never even heard of it! It's banana ice cream with chocolate chunks and walnuts."

"*Banana* ice cream? Who would choose banana ice cream as their favourite, and walnuts are *way* too healthy to have in ice cream!"

Rose laughed again. "My guess is that a lot of people feel the same way as you do. OK, so out of the options they do have, shall we order Phish Food or Chocolate Fudge Brownie?"

"Chocolate Fudge Brownie," said Isla, decisively. "And maybe we could eat it in front of a movie?"

"I guess that would depend on the movie . . ."

"What about *Ice Princess*? Have you seen it? It's on Disney Plus. It's really good. It's about this girl who wants to be a professional ice skater."

Rose smiled. "That sounds perfect."

* * *

A couple of hours later and Isla and Rose were valiantly working their way through big bowls of ice cream while the dogs watched them from their spot in front of the fire.

"I don't think I've ever eaten this much," said Rose, rubbing her stomach.

"I'm already looking forward to the leftover pizza for breakfast tomorrow," declared Isla.

"Leftover pizza? For breakfast?" repeated Rose, incredulously.

"Have you never had it? It's the best!"

"I guess I'll find out tomorrow."

"Do you like the movie?"

"I love it. Can we just pause for a minute to take these bowls and things out and get me a cup of tea?"

"Sure," Isla said. "I'll let the dogs outside."

The animals followed them into the kitchen and Isla let them outside while Rose put the kettle on. "Would you like a hot drink?" Rose asked.

"I'll just have some more Pepsi."

They cleared up a bit while they waited for the dogs to finish in the garden. Rose watched Isla putting things back in the fridge and realised how much she was enjoying spending her Saturday night hanging out with her. She was lovely company and it was so nice to have someone to chat to and relax with when she'd been living by herself for so long. For the first time in a while, Rose wasn't lonely. It felt really good.

* * *

When Alastair's taxi pulled up outside the house at six the following evening, he looked exhausted and train-dirty, but couldn't help smiling at how homely it looked with the Christmas trees flanking the door, the fairy lights adorning the house, and light shining out of the downstairs windows. He paid the driver, opened the front door and was greeted by his dogs as he called out, "Hello!".

"We're in here!" he heard Isla shout from the kitchen.

He entered the warm, bright room to find his daughter sitting at the table peeling carrots. He paused momentarily. He'd never seen Isla take an interest in any kind of cooking before.

Rose turned and smiled at him as she checked something in the oven. Her hair was messy and pulled up in a bun. Her cheeks flushed from the heat of the oven.

"Hi, Dad," said Isla, looking up. "Rose is cooking us a roast!"

"Welcome back," Rose said. "I thought you might be hungry after your trip."

"Thank you, I am." He found himself unable to move from the doorway or tear his eyes away from her. "You didn't have to do that."

"I fancied cooking," said Rose, with a shrug. "How was your weekend?"

"Tiring, it's good to be home." He smiled. "But the meeting did prove to be worthwhile."

"There's time for you to have a shower to freshen up before it's ready if you'd like. You've got at least half an hour."

"Thank you, that would be good, actually."

He went upstairs somehow feeling like a weight had been lifted off his shoulders. It had been a long weekend, the meeting had gone well but all he'd wanted was to be at home with his daughter, and, well, Rose he now realised, if he were to be completely honest with himself. It had felt so good to walk into his bright, warm house and to be greeted by them both and not to have to immediately sort out something to eat for himself and Isla, which would probably have been beans on toast. It definitely wouldn't have been something that smelled anywhere near as good as what Rose was making. A roast was what he really fancied. Perfect on this cold, dark evening.

He hurried his shower, subconsciously wanting to return to the cosy scene in the kitchen. Once he'd dressed and come back downstairs, he took a detour down to the cellar to get a bottle of wine.

Rose was taking a beautifully cooked piece of beef out of the oven when he came back into the kitchen and Isla was nowhere to be seen.

"She's just gone to finish packing her school bag for tomorrow," Rose explained.

"Oh good," said Alastair. Another thing he didn't need to do tonight it seemed was to nag his daughter to get ready for the morning . . .

"I was going to open some wine if you'd like a glass," he said. "It's a Merlot, but I can get you some white if you'd prefer?"

"No, red sounds good. Thank you," Rose said.

Alastair got out two wine glasses and poured for them both. He handed one to Rose, who took a sip. "It's delicious," she declared, causing Alastair to smile.

"Thank you again for this weekend. It was really good to know that Isla was having such a good time. She's always miserable when she has to come to London with me."

"I would have thought she'd love to go?"

69

"She would if it wasn't for business. But I'm usually so busy in meetings or preparing for meetings that there's not much time for us to do much sightseeing. Plus, she was really looking forward to this weekend. She sounded so happy about the match. Thanks for the video of her goal."

"You're welcome — it was pure luck that I happened to be filming then." Rose laughed.

Isla returned and Alastair helped Rose to serve up the roast beef, Yorkshire puddings, crispy roast potatoes, stuffing, gravy, broccoli and carrots that she'd cooked.

"This looks fantastic," he said. "I'm starving."

"Nearly forgot the horseradish sauce," said Rose, putting it on the table.

They dug into the food.

"Wow, Rose this is as good as Mrs Reed's cooking!" declared Isla.

"High accolade indeed!" Rose said with a grin.

"It is really good," agreed Alastair. "Are the Yorkshires homemade?"

"Of course!" replied Rose, mock indignantly. "My mother would never forgive me if I served up ready-made ones!"

"So did your mum teach you to cook?" Isla asked.

Alastair immediately switched his attention to his daughter, checking she was all right as he always did whenever someone's mother was mentioned.

"She did," said Rose carefully, and Alastair found his attention divided between the two of them. There was something not quite right about the expression on Rose's face.

"So, tell me about your day, Isla. How was Lucy's birthday trip?" Alastair asked, wanting to change the subject.

"It was great!" said Isla. "Her mum hired out the whole cinema for us to watch *Star Wars: A New Hope* and we ate so much popcorn."

"That does sound really good," said Alastair. "What did you get up to while madam here was in the cinema, Rose?"

"Oh, Rose was invited to stay," Isla piped up. "All the parents were, but they sat at the back of the cinema, near the bar."

"I didn't have an alcoholic drink," Rose quickly clarified.

"Don't worry," said Alastair. "I trust you completely with my daughter."

And he found he did. Even though he'd only known this woman for a little over a week.

CHAPTER 8

The next few days flew by for Rose as she continued organising the first of the big Christmas events. In a way, this was actually the more stressful one even though the second was undoubtedly fancier and of more importance. This was Rose's first opportunity to prove herself.

She thought the downstairs looked great, but she wasn't completely sure Alastair had really noticed any of the decorations she'd put up apart from the Christmas tree he'd been forced to comment on. Which was fine. He didn't care about Christmas or about how the house was decorated, she could more than understand that. But he would care that his event went without a hitch and that his employees enjoyed themselves.

An entire day was taken up with wrapping all of the presents she'd bought for everyone who worked for Alastair in some capacity on his estate – thirty-six people in total. Obviously she didn't know everyone, but she'd got advice from Mairi and Mrs Reed and had done her best to get each employee something they'd like. And she'd been instructed by Alastair to get Mairi something special as well as a gift for her baby.

She turned the big table in the library into wrapping central, and she'd already warned Alastair that he would need to come and sign all the cards she'd also written out. It would be helpful if she could move the presents under the tree after she'd finished wrapping each one, but she didn't trust the dogs not to investigate.

She heard Alastair arrive home with Isla the day before the first event. He'd been in meetings all day and had picked her up on his way home.

"Hello, Mrs Reed, hello Rose," called out Isla.

"Hello!" called out Mrs Reed from the kitchen.

Rose came out into the hallway. "Hi, Isla. Did you have a good day at school?"

"Pretty good. Physics was a bit boring. I've got some homework to do." Isla glanced through into the library. "Will there be room for me to join you?"

"Sure," Rose said, smiling. "I'm almost done with the wrapping and can clear most of it away now. You are going to have to help me convince your dad to come in and sign all the Christmas cards."

Isla laughed. "Good luck with that one!" she said.

"I said I'd do it and I will," the man in question said with a sigh.

"The party's tomorrow . . ." Rose pointed out.

"I know . . ."

"And there's no time like the present. They're all set out in a pile for you. All you have to do is sign."

"You could just forge my signature," Alastair suggested. "I can get you a copy."

Rose glared at him.

"Fine," he said. "Can I at least get changed first?"

"You can. I'll even make you a cup of coffee which will be waiting for you in the library," Rose offered.

"Okay, I'll be down soon," Alastair said.

"I wouldn't trust him," remarked Isla, making both adults laugh.

"I'll be less than five minutes," Alastair said. "You can time me if you like."

"I don't believe that will be necessary," said Rose . . . noticing Isla clocking the time on her phone.

* * *

True to his word, Alastair was back downstairs just a few minutes later. He was wearing one of his thick wool jumpers and a pair of faded blue jeans.

"Thank you," said Rose, handing him the pile of cards and a pen and turning back to the last of the wrapping.

"No, thank *you*," said Alastair. "It looks like you've done a brilliant job."

"I guess we'll see what people think tomorrow!"

"Are you nervous?" Alastair asked.

"A little," admitted Rose.

"I'm sure it will go brilliantly."

"It'll be really busy around here from about midday . . ." Rose explained.

"So you'd prefer it if I kept out of the way?"

"Exactly." Rose grinned.

"I'll be at my offices on the far side of the estate until after five."

"Perfect." Rose giggled as Alastair shook his head in mock despair.

Isla came in to join them with her homework and the three fell into silence, each absorbed in their tasks, until Alastair breathed a sigh of relief and handed the signed cards back to Rose.

"May I be released from service?" he asked.

"Do I have to check them or can I trust that you signed them all and not just the ones at the top and bottom?"

Alastair laughed. "I solemnly swear that I signed every single one of those cards."

"Then, yes, you may go," agreed Rose.

"You two are so funny," Isla voiced, looking between the two adults who smiled at each other awkwardly.

* * *

Nerves kept Rose awake for most of the night and she was up early feeling rather sick. She showered and made her way downstairs to the kitchen, thinking a cup of tea might revive her.

Mrs Reed was already hard at work as usual, though Rose had made sure there wouldn't be anything extra she had to do for the event.

"Rough night?" she asked, kindly. She placed a mug of tea in front of Rose, doing her usual trick of knowing exactly what someone needed.

"A bit," admitted Rose. "I just really hope tonight goes well."

"I'm sure it will. You've worked so hard and the house looks absolutely wonderful."

"Thank you."

"Here you go, to keep your strength up for the duration," Mrs Reed said, putting a plate full of food down in front of Rose.

"Oh, thank you, but I'm so nervous, I'll never be able to eat all this!" Rose looked down at the sausages, bacon, scrambled eggs, fried tomatoes, baked beans, mushrooms and fried bread.

"You just eat whatever you can manage." Mrs Reed squeezed Rose's shoulder.

"I hope there's some left for me," Alastair quipped as he entered the kitchen.

"There is," said Mrs Reed. "Not that you'll be working as hard as Rose today, but still . . ."

Alastair laughed. "A fair comment."

He sat down opposite Rose and began to eat from the plate Mrs Reed passed him.

"Are you all set for tonight?" he asked.

"I hope so! I'm picking the suit you wanted to wear up from the dry cleaners later this morning, by the way."

"Excellent, thank you. And are you all sorted for something to wear? Did you bring something suitable from London? You know it's not black tie or anything . . ."

"I mean, obviously, I'm going to be here to keep an eye on things and will dress appropriately. I'll be in the background and on hand to sort out anything that needs sorting. I'll likely stay out of the way in the kitchen if all is running smoothly . . ."

"Don't be silly!" Alistair put his knife and fork down. "You have to attend   properly attend! I always meant you to," he declared.

"Absolutely," agreed Mrs Reed, nodding away . . . and now with hands on hips.

"This party is for everyone who works for me to have a night where they can relax and let their hair down. I expect your hair to be let down as well. Unless you'd rather wear it up, of course," Alastair said, sounding flustered.

"That's really nice of you," Rose said. "But what if something goes wrong . . ."

"I doubt it will. It sounds like you've organised everything brilliantly, but if it does then you'll be right here. The catering staff will be able to find you easily enough."

"I suppose."

"Have you got something you can wear?" asked Mrs Reed.

"Yes . . ." said Rose, remembering the little black cocktail dress she'd packed and brought with her just in case.

"Perfect then," said Alastair, smiling. "Because, frankly, if I have to go to this thing then I see no reason why you should be able to get out of it!"

* * *

The day flew by as Rose went out to pick up Alastair's suit and some last-minute bits she'd thought of. She arrived back in plenty of time to have a cup of tea and check her to-do list before she began moving around the furniture.

Mac, the gardener, had been engaged to bring down all the extra chairs from the attic as well as a bunch of little tables and to help clear as much furniture out of the way as possible. The dining room table was extended as far as it would go and that, along with some extra trolleys provided by the caterers would be where the buffet would be served. People could then eat in there or in the drawing room. The library was set up with a bar and as a quieter place for people who wanted to talk, away from the noise of the music and later the karaoke machine.

The aim of this event was for people to relax and just have a great night out with their work friends. Rose was a tiny bit concerned about people getting carried away with all the free drinks, but she hoped that Alastair's presence would put a stop to that. Alastair's company was paying for taxis home for all the guests so no one had to worry about driving. She guessed if anyone did get too inebriated, they could just be subtly popped into a taxi early.

The caterers arrived and soon it was non-stop busy with the kitchen, drawing room, dining room and library being completely taken over by them. Rose was glad she had her room as a sanctuary from the madness and a place she could go to hide for a minute to recalibrate. She did a little sketching to calm her nerves during the moments she wasn't needed. The DJ and the karaoke machine arrived and set up in the drawing room.

There should be plenty of room for everyone, she thought, relieved that it was all coming together. She hoped it would be a fun night and everyone would be happy with the change of format. Usually they had a meal in a restaurant and there was sometimes dancing afterwards. From what Mairi had told her, it appeared that everyone was usually home and tucked up in their beds by 10 p.m., which sounded pretty tame for a Christmas party. But had she gone too far in the other direction?

But then what could she do? It wasn't like she had a lot of options when she'd been asked to organise this party only a couple of weeks ago. Considering what was available to her at such a late date, she thought she'd done a really great job. Fingers crossed everyone else, especially Alastair, agreed.

* * *

Mrs Reed had left at lunchtime as there were going to be so many people milling around and there wouldn't be anything left for her to do. She'd hugged Rose before she left. "It'll be brilliant," she whispered in her ear. Mrs Reed would be returning later on, along with her husband, as guests to the event itself.

Isla wasn't around either as she was having a sleepover at her friend Lucy's house.

* * *

The party was due to start at seven and everything was going smoothly so Rose escaped upstairs to get changed at six. She thanked past-Rose for remembering to pack shoes to go with her dress.

Her cocktail dress was a favourite and made her feel a little like Audrey Hepburn with its high boat-line neck and flared skirt. She hoped she still looked professional enough despite the fact that she was showing quite a bit of leg. Well, she thought, she didn't have anything else to wear, so this would have to do. She reapplied her make-up, following a YouTube tutorial to give herself *flawless skin and sultry eyes*, and was quite pleased with the results. Finally, she used a curling iron on her hair to create some soft curls around her face, and declared herself fit for the evening.

She was downstairs again half an hour before guests were due and reached the entrance hall just as Alastair came in the front door. The expression on his face as he looked around his home, taken over by Christmas and caterers, was priceless and Rose wished she'd been able to save it for posterity. Isla would have found it hilarious.

It took Alastair a moment to notice Rose amid the hustle and bustle. His eyes widened slightly at the sight of her and he seemed to momentarily lose the power of speech.

"Perfect timing," she said, breaking the tension. "Do you need anything before you head upstairs to change?"

"Um, no, thank you, I'll just . . . I'll see you in a bit . . ." He hurried past her, taking the stairs two at a time.

That was interesting, Rose thought to herself. She hadn't expected a dress to receive that much of a reaction. She tried and failed to hide the smile on her face as she proceeded to check in with everyone and ensure that all was ready for when the guests arrived.

* * *

The party was in full swing and everyone seemed to be having a great time. She caught glimpses of Alastair now and again, looking almost impossibly handsome with the top button of his shirt undone, but he seemed to be doing an excellent job of keeping out of her way. At least he was still here, she consoled herself.

Rose had so far spent most of the evening, when she wasn't busy making sure that everything was running smoothly, with Mairi, who'd introduced herself as soon as she'd arrived with her husband, Mark. Mairi was just as lovely as Rose had imagined she would be and it was nice to have someone to talk to so she didn't feel like a wallflower.

Once the food was eaten and out of the way, people began to dance. Mrs Reed had returned to the house with her husband and was the life and soul of the party, much to Rose's delight.

Alastair was then conspicuous by his absence. Rose wandered around, checking everything was okay and that everyone was enjoying themselves. As she suspected, no one was getting too carried away with the drink, having their boss at the party with them was having the desired effect.

She did start to wonder where Alastair had gone though. She gave him half an hour and then sent him a text asking, "*Are you in hiding?*" and put her phone back in the kitchen drawer. Stupid women's clothes with no pockets, she thought.

She wandered back out to the party and was watching Mrs Reed and Mac busting some moves on the dance floor, when she felt a tap on her shoulder and turned around to find herself facing Alastair. He must have realised how close they were because he took a little step back.

He handed her a glass of wine.

"Thank you," Rose said. "But I'm not drinking while I'm working. My boss might see." She grinned.

"Everything's fine," said Alastair, returning the smile. "People have eaten. The caterers are almost packed up. I've tipped them and they're going to email the invoice. You're officially off duty and it's time for you to enjoy yourself. I've asked that any problems be brought to me to deal with. Not that there will be any problems," he added, noticing the worried look crossing Rose's face. "You've worked really hard and everyone's having a great time. It's time for you to properly relax."

"Thank you," she said and took a sip of wine and then stopped. "What is this? This isn't what we've been serving I tasted that a few days ago."

"That's a little something special," said Alastair, with a wink.

"It's really good."

"I'm glad you like it."

The song ended and the DJ announced that karaoke would begin in just a few moments.

Alastair's face fell as he turned to Rose. "Did he just say what I think he did? Karaoke?"

"He did, I'm afraid." Rose struggled not to laugh.

"I don't like you very much right now," Alastair announced as Mrs Reed marched up to the microphone and declared she was going to sing 'Bohemian Rhapsody' with her husband.

"I understand that," said Rose, as solemnly as she could manage.

"I can't believe you didn't warn me!"

"Can you blame me?"

"I suppose not . . ."

They stood and watched the performers for a while.

"Admit it, everyone loves it," said Rose smugly.

"Not everyone," muttered Alastair.

"So, were you hiding upstairs before you came to bring me this wine?" Rose asked.

"No!" Alastair said, indignantly. "I was in the wine cellar, choosing the wine for you."

"For how long?" asked Rose, narrowing her eyes.

"Maybe a little longer than was strictly necessary."

Rose gave a roll of her eyes. "I'm glad you decided to come back."

"I got your message and figured I'd been rumbled." He shrugged as he looked at his feet.

"I didn't even know you had a wine cellar so I wouldn't have thought to check it. You probably could have got away with hiding out down there for a little while longer."

"I should have thought of that."

Mrs Reed appeared seemingly out of nowhere and thrust a microphone into Alastair's hand. "You're up!" she said, firmly and loudly enough for everyone around them to hear.

"Oh no, not me," said Alastair, backing away while simultaneously attempting to give the microphone back. He looked absolutely petrified.

Mrs Reed put her hands behind her back and Alastair frantically tried to pass it to Rose who wouldn't take it. "The karaoke was your idea!" he said.

"I thought I'd be working!"

Mrs Reed signalled to her husband who brought over another microphone and handed it to her.

"You can do a duet," Mrs Reed declared, taking advantage of their shock to thrust the second microphone at Rose. "I think 'Don't Go Breaking My Heart' will do perfectly." The other guests let out a cheer.

Alastair and Rose found themselves gently shoved towards their fate.

* * *

"I can't believe I did that," said Alastair. He and Rose were hiding in the wine cellar, recovering from their ordeal with the rest of the special bottle of wine. They sat on the floor with their backs to the wall.

"We were *dreadful*. Truly dreadful," laughed Rose. "I'm going to be having flashbacks for years."

"I'm charging Mrs Reed for my therapy sessions. I don't care that she's practically family and has been housekeeper here since before I was born," Alastair muttered.

"I've got to ask, do you know her first name? Or is it a mystery to you as well?" Rose queried.

"It's Carol," mock whispered Alastair. "But I've never dared call her that to her face."

"I don't blame you . . . Carol . . ." Rose tried out the name. "I think she'll always be Mrs Reed to me."

"Me too," Alastair admitted. "And not just because I'm genuinely scared of what her reaction would be if I called her Carol."

"Come on," said Rose getting up from the floor. "We'd better get back to the fun."

"Do we have to?" asked Alastair. "I doubt anyone would notice if I didn't go back."

"Yes, they would!" she said, hauling him to his feet, trying not to notice that his hand was more calloused than she'd imagined. She knew from Mrs Reed that he usually spent part of his working week actually on the estate tending to the animals and the land, presumably that was the cause. "Come on. It's cold in here."

"I should have offered you my jacket," Alastair said.

"I'm fine." Rose grinned. "It'll be over soon. The taxis are coming to pick everyone up in under half an hour."

Rose reached the cellar door and felt Alastair hang back. "Your torture is so nearly ended," she said, taking hold of his hand again to pull him along behind her.

Just then the cellar door opened and Mrs Reed stood in front of them. She looked from Rose to Alastair. Her confusion was clear.

"Mrs Reed, hello," said Alastair, overly brightly.

"What on earth are you both doing in the wine cellar?" asked Mrs Reed, glancing from one to the other like they'd been caught smoking behind the bike shed. "I saw the light was on and thought I heard voices. I didn't expect to find you two though!"

"We were just getting some wine . . ." Rose mumbled, holding up the near-empty bottle she had in her hand.

"Better get back to the party," Alastair said, briskly.

Mrs Reed moved to the side.

Alastair and Rose scurried off in the direction of the library. Rose didn't dare catch Alastair's eye in case she burst into a fit of giggles.

"Oh dear," she said when they were well out of Mrs Reed's earshot.

"I don't think I've been given that look since she caught me attempting to make my own fireworks in the workshop when I was about eleven."

"We'd better behave ourselves for the rest of the evening."

"Agreed. I'll do a final round of the party chatting to everyone," Alastair said.

"Great, I'll see you later."

Rose wandered around herself, checking in with the bar staff and just generally making sure that everything was winding down well. She watched Alastair out of the corner of her eye. She could tell now that she knew him better that he wasn't completely comfortable in his suit. What might initially come across as standoffish to an outside observer was actually that he'd rather be in one of his thick wool jumpers chatting to his daughter in the kitchen while sipping a cup of tea. He wasn't a natural in a suit, even if he did look really good in one.

Rose breathed a sigh of relief at midnight when the taxis began to arrive and people fetched their coats and started to leave. It had been a great evening and she was so glad it had been a success; she was very ready for it to be over though.

She waited by the front door, saying goodbye and thanking everybody for coming and handing out the presents. She was joined by Alastair when she managed to catch his attention and convey through a glare that this was also where he needed to be.

When she saw Mrs Reed and her husband approaching, she glanced frantically around for an escape route, but there was none, there were too many people milling about.

"Good night, Mrs Reed, Mr Reed," she said pleasantly, plastering a smile upon her face. "I hope you've had a good evening."

"We've had a wonderful time, thank you," said Mr Reed, beaming.

"Yes," said Mrs Reed. "A lovely evening. You must be exhausted and anxious to get into your bed. And sleep," she finished pointedly.

"Absolutely," agreed Rose, trying to keep a straight face.

Mrs Reed threw Rose and Alastair one last anxious look before leaving with a somehow ominous sounding, "I'll see you bright and early Monday morning."

Rose fought not to make eye contact with Alastair. She knew that would be her undoing and she wouldn't be able to help laughing. "See you then," she managed to say keeping a fairly straight face.

When the last of the guests had left, Alastair turned to Rose and said, "Are you going to bed now?"

"I think it might be a good idea to hang around until the bar staff and the DJ have finished packing up . . ."

"I'd forgotten about them," said Alastair with a little sigh. "Would you like a nightcap with me while they work?"

"Sure," said Rose, with a carefully nonchalant shrug. There was nothing for her to do other than wait for people to be ready to leave anyway.

"I'll get some whisky and meet you in the sitting room," he said.

"Okay."

Rose let the DJ and the bartenders know where she would be when they were done and then joined Alastair who was lighting the fire.

She collapsed into one of the two armchairs facing the fire and pulled the blanket resting on the arm over to cover her. She closed her eyes for a moment and allowed herself to decompress. She opened them as she heard Alastair pouring the drinks. He passed her one. "This whisky is from a distillery near here," he said as he sat down in the chair next to hers and took a sip.

Rose tried the drink and felt the amber liquid travel down her throat, soothing and warming it.

"It's good. Do you own the distillery?" Rose asked, making him smile. He was extremely attractive in the firelight.

"I hope to soon. That's what last weekend's meeting was about."

Rose shook her head. "You know your life isn't exactly normal, don't you?"

Alastair nodded. "I'm aware of how lucky I am. Even on nights like tonight."

"I'm sorry you hated it," said Rose.

"That's not your fault. You did a fantastic job putting this on so last minute. I'm just not the most sociable of creatures."

"Your home will be completely back to normal very soon," comforted Rose.

"Until next Saturday . . ."

"That will all be outside," she reminded him. "I've even hired posh Portaloos so no one needs to come into the house except the caterers to use the kitchen, though they do a lot in their van."

Alastair laughed. "I'm sorry I'm so awkward."

"It's your home, you can be as awkward as you want," she said with a shrug. "And if you'd rather I tried to stay out of your hair more when you're home in the evenings . . ."

"No! No, not at all," said Alastair quickly. Their eyes met, momentarily sending a warm buzz through Rose before he looked away and focused on his glass. "I want you to think of this as your home while you're here, and . . . Isla and I like having you around."

"I like being here. You have a beautiful home and you know I think Isla is amazing."

"She's definitely that . . ."

"You've done a fantastic job bringing her up."

"Thank you," Alastair said slowly. "Honestly, it hasn't always been easy but she's more than worth it."

There was a knock at the sitting room door. "Come in," called out Alastair, and the DJ opened the door.

"I'm about to head off and I think the other guys are too," he said.

"Excellent, I'll come and see you out," said Rose, getting up from her seat.

"You stay there," said Alastair, placing a hand gently on her arm, producing another buzz. "I'll sort this out, you're exhausted."

Rose knew she should protest, this being part of her job after all, but she really was tired, so she nodded and said, "Thank you."

CHAPTER 9

Rose woke the next morning still in her cocktail dress from the night before, but underneath the duvet on her bed. Her shoes had been removed and placed neatly by the side of the bed. She almost trod on them as she stood up.

Alastair must have carried her to her room, she realised. Oh my goodness, how embarrassing and unprofessional! She'd been supposed to be organising an event for him and had ended up falling asleep on duty after drinking his whisky!

She headed to the bathroom, noticing that Alastair's bedroom door was open and his bed made. She showered and dressed, taking her time so she could avoid facing Alastair for as long as possible. Finally, her rumbling stomach, now used to eating a proper breakfast every day, demanded to be fed, so she made her way downstairs like a prisoner off to their execution.

She gave a sigh of relief when she entered the kitchen and saw he was nowhere around. The kettle was still warm though. Maybe he'd gone out?

She put the kettle on to boil again and popped a couple of slices of bread in the toaster.

She was spreading peanut butter on her toast when Alastair came in through the back door with the dogs, making her jump. He rubbed his hands together to warm them up as the dogs came over to say good morning to her.

"I've just been checking on Houdini. It's cold out there," he said, conversationally.

"It looks it," replied Rose.

"Stick a slice in for me, would you?" he said.

"Sure." Rose was careful to avoid eye contact as she put another piece of bread into the toaster.

"Did you sleep well?" Alastair asked, an air of fake non-chalance in his tone.

Rose readied herself and turned to face him. "I'm really sorry about last night. I can't believe I fell asleep . . ."

"You were exhausted," Alastair said kindly as he reboiled the kettle for himself.

"You should have just woken me up . . ."

"You were fast asleep and looked so peaceful. It's not like you weigh a lot, you're tiny."

"It's not that . . ."

Alastair looked aghast. "I didn't mean to make you feel uncomfortable. I just carried you up to your bed, took off your shoes, and put the cover over you so you didn't get cold."

"Oh, no, no, it's just I'm embarrassed. I was supposed to be working and you're my employer . . ."

"I'd already told you, you were off duty and we're also housemates at the moment," Alastair reassured, gently.

Rose smiled. "Okay, well, thank you for looking after me."

"Really, it wasn't a problem. I was even going upstairs myself," he added with a grin, making Rose laugh. "Do you want to come out with me, Houdini and the dogs when you're finished eating? I was going to take them for a walk before picking up Isla."

"Sure," said Rose. It was a dry day for once and the sun was even trying to pop out from behind the clouds. The fresh air would do her good and the cleaners weren't due to arrive to finish the clean-up operation until after lunch.

* * *

Rose made sure she was well bundled up for their walk, and put on as many layers as she could fit underneath her coat. Scotland was definitely colder than London, that was for sure.

Alastair was waiting with the dogs and goat as promised.

"I thought we'd hop in the car and I'd take you to some woods I like. It's not far and we can pick up Isla on the way home."

"Sounds good," said Rose as they walked to the car.

"The looks I get when I'm walking with Houdini are so embarrassing but can you imagine how much trouble I'd be in if I left him at home?"

"You'd be in a lot of trouble," confirmed Rose. "Much easier just to put up with some funny glances."

Alastair put the animals in the car while Rose climbed into the passenger seat, wondering whether it had been such a good idea to accept Alastair's offer. What if he was planning to walk for twenty miles or something? She should have checked.

Just a few minutes later they parked up by a gate that formed the entrance to the woods.

"There are several trails that zigzag through these woods. Isla and I did all of them last summer. The one I'm going to take you on is probably our favourite."

Rose took a deep breath as she got out of the car. The air smelt delicious and piney, which made her smile. How had she ended up here, walking through a remote Scottish woodland with a man whose amazing house she was living and working in?

"Not too cold?" Alastair asked.

"Nope."

"Good, I'm not sure you could have fitted any more clothes on anyway."

Rose laughed. "Better to be safe than sorry. I'm not used to Scottish winters, remember."

Alastair let the animals out of the car.

"These woods aren't more of your estate, are they?" Rose asked.

"No. This one's owned by the Woodland Trust." He pointed to a sign on the gate.

"But you do own woodland?"

"I do," Alastair said, attaching Houdini's lead to his collar.

"What's it like being a laird then?"

"Mostly quite unexciting I'm afraid." Alastair opened the gate and held it for Rose and the dogs to go through.

"It's a big responsibility," Rose commented.

"It is," he agreed. "I feel a duty towards my tenants, and of course to the animals we farm, but I suppose it's what I've always known. My family has held our land for a very long time."

"Do you ever wish you did something else?"

"No," Alastair mused. "I'm not a natural with the animals like my father was, but I have a brilliant estate manager and I've built up the business and maintained the estate. Honestly, I've loved doing it."

"Will Isla take over the estate eventually?"

"Only if she wants to. I wouldn't force her. Fiona never had any interest in staying here. She was off to London and then Manchester as soon as she could, but I belong on the estate."

"Agreed," said Rose. "You look quite out of place anywhere else."

"You noticed, eh?"

"I noticed," Rose confirmed with a smile.

They walked and talked with Houdini trotting along beside them on a lead. The dogs' tails didn't stop wagging for the whole walk. Rose appreciated that no part of this amble was as steep as the hill she climbed with Isla, but the views were still incredible in places. In fact the couple of hours they walked for flew by and Rose was surprised when she spotted the car park and realised they were nearly done.

They piled into the car with three very muddy animals and drove to Isla's friend Lucy's house.

"I'll be back in a minute," Alastair said, opening the car door.

Rose watched him walk up and knock on the front door which was quickly opened by Lucy's mum, Sarah. Who happened to be wearing rather a low cut top despite how cold it was. She leant against the door and flicked her red hair as she chatted to Alastair.

Rose knew she shouldn't be spying but she couldn't help but watch the interaction. It was some relief, not that she wanted to think about why it was a relief, that Alastair could not have looked more uncomfortable. Finally, Isla appeared at the door with her rucksack and Sarah had to move to let her pass.

Alastair and Isla turned towards the car. "Rose!" Isla cried out, waving at the car. Rose saw the scowl on Sarah's face before she closed the front door.

"Did you have a good time?" Rose asked Isla as she climbed into the car and greeted Houdini.

"Yeah! It was great, but I think Lucy's mum really wanted to come to your party, Dad. She kept talking about it."

"She's coming to the event next weekend," said Alastair. "Sarah's my accountant so doesn't work for the company," he explained to Rose. "I thought it made more sense to invite her to the other evening."

"She showed me the dress she's going to wear. I think she fancies you, Dad."

"I think you are a mischief maker," said Alastair with a laugh as he started the car.

"Dad . . ." said Isla, a few minutes later. Rose immediately suspected she'd been building up to asking whatever it was she was about to launch into.

"What are you after?" Alastair asked.

"What makes you think I'm after anything?" asked Isla innocently.

"Oh, so, you're not wanting something from me . . ."

"I didn't say that . . ." Isla said, making the adults laugh.

"What can I do for you, darling daughter?"

"Well," began Isla. "School breaks up on Wednesday and I wondered if I could have some friends round for an end-of-term thing . . ."

"How many friends?" asked Alastair, suspiciously.

"Lucy, obviously, and Charmaine, Emily, Lizzy and Bethan. Not a sleepover but a cool evening thing."

"Six of you in total?" confirmed Alastair.

"Yep," said Isla, hopefully.

"That sounds doable," he said.

"Hooray!"

"What do you want to do? The cinema and then come back to the house?"

"We went to the cinema for Lucy's birthday so I'd rather do something different."

"I can organise it if you like," offered Rose. "It's a Christmas event, so officially it falls under my remit."

"Really?" asked Isla. "That would be so cool!"

"Are you quite sure?" asked Alastair, shooting her a concerned look. "I mean, it's certainly not in your contract and I wouldn't expect . . ."

"It's fine, I'd like to do it. Let me have a think, Isla and we can plan something awesome."

"Cool!"

"Can we make a bit of a detour on the way back?" Rose asked.

"Sure," Alastair said. "Where to?"

"Just follow my directions."

* * *

Fifteen minutes later, they arrived at the Christmas tree farm.

"What are we doing here?" asked Isla.

"It was such a shame you couldn't choose the trees with us, I wondered if you'd like to pick one for your room."

"I'd love to! That would be so cool!" said Isla, excitedly. "But . . . do you think we could put it in the library? That way we can both see it when you're working and I'm helping you or doing my homework in there."

Rose turned to Alastair to check that was okay. "Fine by me," he said. "Though I can't believe I have to strap yet another tree to the roof of this poor car. Nothing bigger than 6 feet! I'm not dealing with another botanical monster."

They wandered around the farm while Isla took her time choosing. It was freezing, but Rose barely noticed as she watched how happy Isla was.

The tree she finally decided on was, honestly, a lopsided runt. Isla's good nature had naturally led her to choose a tree she felt sorry for.

Alastair had the bright idea to stop at a Tesco they passed and Isla managed to find decorations pink and glittery enough to satisfy even her extremely girly tastes.

Rose planned to leave father and daughter to set up and decorate the tree when they got home, but they both asked her to help. Rose was touched and, of course, she joined in, even though it wasn't easy for three people to hang objects on such a small tree at the same time.

In its pot and decorated, the tree was no straighter or less spindly, but Isla was thrilled.

"Thank you," said Alastair mouthed to Rose as Isla hugged her and told her yet again how much she loved her Christmas tree.

* * *

Rose used the time the cleaners were working later that afternoon to come up with some fun things for Isla to choose from. The little flat in which she'd grown up, and still lived in, was never big enough to host five friends, but she would have loved to have been able to and she really wanted Isla to have a good time.

Alastair brought her a hot drink while she was googling ideas.

"Thank you," she said.

"No problem, thanks for doing this for Isla. She's so excited."

"I thought she might like to go bowling . . ." Rose said. "There's a bowling alley not too far from her school."

"And there's a burger place next door to it which she loves. We could take them there for food afterwards," Alastair suggested.

"I think she'd like that," Rose said. She certainly would have done at that age.

"And then back here I guess to play some of their K-pop and paint their nails or whatever it is they like to do when they get together."

"Maybe we could do an ice cream bar for them and set them all up with pamper kits?" Rose suggested. "That should keep them busy."

"She is going to absolutely love that. We'll need to use both cars . . ."

Rose nodded. "Why do you have a spare Land Rover, by the way?"

"They're quite temperamental . . . it pays to have a backup."

Rose laughed. "Fair enough. And, yes, I can manage some of the girls and you take the others."

"Shall we tell her what's planned or keep it as a surprise?"

"Definitely a surprise. We'll just ask the parents to pick up from our house at like ten?"

"Sounds good. Thanks for organising it all."

"It's an absolute pleasure," said Rose.

* * *

Rose was dreading facing Mrs Reed on Monday morning. It had been embarrassing being caught in the cellar with Alastair, not that there had been anything going on of course. They were just friends. She smiled at that thought. When she'd first met Alastair just over two weeks ago, there was no way she would have thought they would ever be friends. They just seemed so different. But now she was getting to know the real Alastair and she liked him.

She waited as long as possible before going downstairs, planning to take her breakfast into the library and to start work straight away.

Mrs Reed was in the kitchen when Rose entered. Rose steeled herself and said, cheerfully, "Good morning."

"Good morning," Mrs Reed replied, in nothing like her usual tone. She sounded more quiet . . . Subdued? "I trust you enjoyed the rest of your weekend." She didn't look up from the dishwasher which she was unloading and this was probably the longest Rose had been in the kitchen with Mrs Reed without being offered a hot drink. Something was definitely up.

"I did, thank you," she replied tentatively.

"Isla tells me you went to pick her up from her friend's house and that you and Mr Duncan cooked together."

"We did, yes," Rose admitted, desperately trying not to smile at the memory of the lovely cosy evening she, Isla and Alastair had spent cooking and hanging out together. The mammoth game of Monopoly last night had been a particular highlight. But she was sobered by the fact that she could practically feel the disapproval radiating off Mrs Reed.

"Alastair's been very kind trying to make me feel welcome and not too homesick," Rose said.

Mrs Reed finally turned to Rose. "You're only going to be here for another couple of weeks. I know he's handsome, and I've noticed the way he looks at you, but . . . Mr Duncan has been hurt before and I don't want to see him hurt again," she said gently but firmly.

"There's nothing going on between the two of us," Rose managed to say, reeling from Mrs Reed's little revelation that Alastair looked at her . . . did he? Was Mrs Reed just imagining things? Or was there some truth in what she said? "We're just friends. You know Ala— Mr Duncan doesn't like parties. He was hiding away in the wine cellar and I was bringing him back to join everyone when you saw us. That's all."

Mrs Reed didn't appear entirely convinced but seemed willing to at least consider that what Rose was saying was true.

"He's a good man . . ." said Mrs Reed.

"He is," said Rose. "But he's also my boss."

Mrs Reed nodded. A truce of sorts had been declared. She patted Rose on the arm. "You must be gasping for a cuppa. What can I get you?"

* * *

Happier now that things were back on an even keel with Mrs Reed, Rose took her coffee through to the library and opened up her laptop to start work. There was going to be plenty to do with the Christmas dinner event on Saturday and Alastair's family arriving the day before. Isla's little gathering was another thing now on her plate, but that shouldn't take up much time. The bowling alley was booked as well as two tables at the burger place next door, one for the girls and one for Rose and Alastair they didn't think the girls would think it very cool for the grown-ups to sit with them. Rose had made sure that the tables were as far apart as possible so that Isla had her space, while Alastair could keep an eye on them. All she needed to sort out was the ice cream and the pampering goodies which she planned to go out for the day before.

Her phone rang and Alastair's name flashed up on the screen.

"Hello," she said, as she answered, unable to help a little smile appearing on her lips.

"Hi, Rose. I wanted to speak to you without Isla around. I need to go shopping for her Christmas presents as well as those for everyone else in my family, to be honest . . . I was going to take the day off tomorrow to do it and I wondered if you'd join me? I mean, if you've got time, of course."

Rose quickly went over in her mind what she needed to do in the next few days . . . It was certainly a busy week and it was a lot, but helping Alastair with his Christmas shopping fell within what she was contracted to do so she could hardly say no . . . She also realised that she really *wanted* to go Christmas shopping with Alastair. She pushed that thought swiftly to the back of her mind.

"I have time," she said. "Everything for Saturday is set up."

"Great! We'll drop Isla off at school tomorrow and drive to Edinburgh from there. And it'll mean you get to see some of the city while you're here."

CHAPTER 10

Isla was most put out to be missing a shopping trip.

"We'd hardly be able to buy your Christmas presents if you came with us, would we?" pointed out Alastair, making Rose laugh.

"I suppose not," admitted Isla.

"And you never know, I might bring you back some of that fudge you love if I so happen to be passing the shop that makes it . . ."

"Fine! You win," said Isla. "As long as I get fudge."

Isla was taken to school, indignant that her goat couldn't come for the drive, but was promised that Mrs Reed and Houdini would pick her up at the end of the day as her dad and Rose probably wouldn't be back in time.

Once Isla got out of the car, Alastair rolled his eyes upwards and turned off her K-pop and put the radio on.

"So, have you got a plan for today?" Rose asked.

"Not really," Alastair admitted. "Isla's easy. She wants a new bike, and then I was hoping you'd help me to choose some bits for her stocking."

"Sounds like another trip to Claire's Accessories."

Alastair groaned. "I hate that place."

Rose laughed. "Isla loves it though and she'll be thrilled with pretty much anything from there."

"The twins are easy to buy for. They both like Lego and there's a big toy shop we can go to for that. Aunt Helena is a bit trickier. There's no point in getting her art supplies I've learned because I never get it right. But she does really like art books, so maybe we could head to Waterstones and see what they've got . . ."

"This is all sounding pretty straightforward so far," said Rose.

"That's because we haven't got to the tricky people yet . . ."

"Oh . . ." said Rose.

"Yeah, I mean, what do I buy Mrs Reed? I want to get her something extra as well as that murder mystery DVD boxset she had at the staff party. She enjoys cooking, but she's my housekeeper so it seems wrong to buy her kitchen stuff."

"Cookery books?" suggested Rose.

"But what if she thinks they're a hint that I don't like her cooking. Or worse, changes some of her recipes? Isla would never forgive me."

"I'm sure we can think of something for her. How about we get some of the easy ones out of the way first?"

"Easy wins sound like a great idea," said Alastair.

They chatted through some more ideas for Christmas presents as they drove.

"Right, where should we start?" asked Rose, once they'd reached the city and found a place to park. She'd been making notes on her phone during the journey and was raring to go. She'd dressed practically in jeans and a hoodie and wore her reliable trainers for dry, non-muddy city walking as well as a coat, hat, scarf and gloves because Scotland really was cold!

Alastair was also in jeans but teamed with a soft, thick knitted jumper, and while he had on a coat, hardened Scotsman that he was, he forewent the accessories.

"Over there I think," said Alastair, pointing to a Costa Coffee.

"Coffee should be a reward for when you've bought at least some presents," Rose suggested.

"I hate shopping and I especially hate Christmas shopping so I say I deserve a reward for getting here. Plus, I'll be good for nothing if I don't have some coffee soon."

"I suspected you were a bit of a coffee addict," confided Rose.

"I used to be a lot worse," he confessed. "But then Mrs Reed weaned me off by replacing some of my coffees with decaf."

"That's so sneaky!"

"She started by mixing decaffeinated coffee in with my caffeinated. The woman's a genius. But the fact remains that I am refusing to do any shopping until I have an espresso."

"Fine," Rose muttered, following him into Costa, which she had to admit, did look very warm and inviting.

Once caffeinated, they made their way to the Lego Store and bought Alastair's twin nephews a giant Lego Star Wars set each. "That should keep them busy for a while," Alastair said.

"They could do them on the big table in the library so the dogs won't get at any of the pieces . . ." Rose suggested. "Actually, where does Houdini usually go for Christmas? Please say you don't take him to your sister's house in Manchester!"

"No," said Alastair, laughing. "This is only his second Christmas. Last year he stayed at an animal sanctuary while we were away, and, personally, it seemed like he had a great time, but Isla was completely miserable. She was worried people would think he wasn't loved and didn't have a home and that the sanctuary staff would allow him to be adopted by mistake. That's one of the main reasons why I agreed to have everyone here this year. I couldn't go through that again. She even wanted to video call him so she could see him opening the presents she'd got him."

"That girl really does love her goat."

"In fairness, I think he feels the same way about her," Alastair said.

Claire's Accessories was close by so they went in there with Alastair looking supremely uncomfortable around all the pink and sparkle.

"It could be worse," Rose said as she helped him choose some hair things for Isla. "This is a serious step-up from the Christmas shop I worked in."

"Of course it's not! Not one member of staff is dressed as a Disney princess sorry, queen."

"Lucky for them," remarked Rose.

"Do you miss London?" Alastair asked.

"No," Rose answered, honestly. "London . . . well, it hasn't felt like home for a while."

Alastair nodded.

"Isla would really like to have her ears pierced you know . . ."

Alastair put his hands up. "Yes, her not-so-subtle hints have not gone unnoticed."

"And?"

"I'll let her do it on her thirteenth birthday," he said with a sigh. "I'm just hoping she forgets about it by then."

"If she's anything like me, she won't," commiserated Rose, putting her hair behind her ears to show the three earrings in each.

"You are such a bad example," he joked.

"I won't tell her about my tattoo," Rose said, with a wink.

"Demands for a tattoo, I'm definitely not ready to deal with! Is it time for us to get lunch yet?"

"No!" said Rose, adamantly. "It's far too early, and not until we've dealt with some of the tough presents."

An hour later they lugged their purchases back to the car and locked them in the boot.

"Now may I have lunch before we head back into the shops?" Alastair asked, looking exhausted. "Surely I've done enough shopping to deserve some sustenance?"

"Fine," said Rose. "But it's already one, so it needs to be something quick. We've still got a fair number of presents to buy."

"There's a Pret A Manger round the corner, will that do?"

"That will do perfectly." Rose smiled. Alastair was a complete wimp when it came to Christmas shopping.

Alastair seemed happy to linger over lunch for as long as possible, but a glare from Rose got him to finish off his drink so they could head out again.

They walked through the city centre, Alastair leading Rose the long way around to the shops they were heading for so she could see more of the city. Edinburgh was decked out beautifully for Christmas, with elaborate fairy lights and Christmas trees adorning the shops, and the window displays glittering on every street.

It was busy with people bustling around each other laden down with shopping, but that seemed to add to the festive feel which was further enhanced by the carol singers they came across.

The German Christmas market was in full swing, and the smell of the roasted chestnuts was irresistible. Alastair got them a packet to share which they demolished in about two minutes flat.

"Oh, wow!" she said as they turned a corner and she caught sight of what was ahead. "Is that an outdoor ice rink?"

"Yeah, I think they set it up every year," said Alastair. "I've brought Isla a few times."

"Can we take a look?"

"Sure."

They walked up to the barriers and watched the skaters. It was quiet as schools hadn't broken up yet.

"It's like something out of a movie set in New York," Rose sighed.

"I think it's a bit smaller than the one at the Rockefeller Center," commented Alastair.

"You know what I mean," said Rose, elbowing him in the ribs. He pretended to double over in pain.

"Come on," he said, taking her hand. "Let's have a go."

"We're supposed to be shopping!" Rose said. "This is just another excuse to get out of finding something for Mrs Reed."

"It's a good excuse though, isn't it," said Alastair, grinning and leading her to the ticket office. "Two tickets, please," he said as they reached the counter.

Rose was incredulous as he paid and was handed their tickets.

"What size skates?" asked the teenage girl with a lip ring running the booth.

"Ten," said Alastair.

"Four," Rose found herself saying. She was handed a pair of white ice skates and followed Alastair over to a bench to put them on.

"Have you skated before?" Alastair asked, standing up.

"Once when I was about eleven."

"I have skated at least three times with Isla. Maybe four. So it appears I'm somewhat of an expert, by comparison at least."

"You're not exactly filling me with confidence."

"It was you who wanted to skate."

"Did I?"

"You wanted to skate," Alastair repeated.

"In theory maybe," said Rose, looking warily down at the ice skates now on her feet.

"You ready?" He held out a hand to her.

"I'm supposed to walk in these things?"

"Just to the rink and then we skate in these things."

"You've got an answer for everything," grumbled Rose, but she accepted his hand and walked like newborn Bambi to the ice.

"This is really slippery," she squeaked as she stepped on the ice and almost lost her footing straight away.

"Hang on to the side until you get your balance," advised Alastair, stepping rather more confidently onto the ice. "It's all a matter of balance . . ." He pushed off with his right foot and made it about a metre before falling on his bum.

* * *

"I am going to be so bruised tomorrow," Rose said as she sat down on the bench an hour later to remove her skates.

"You did brilliantly." Alastair passed her shoes.

"I did not!"

Alastair laughed and shrugged. "You had fun though, right?"

"I did, thank you," Rose replied, completely and utterly honestly.

"Time for another coffee?" suggested Alastair. "Or a mulled wine?" He indicated to a cheerful little, red-painted hut in the Christmas market and raised an eyebrow.

"No!" grinned Rose. "We're here to shop."

* * *

They returned to the house just before five, exhausted and with a car full of presents.

Rose smiled as they approached the house. It was dark and the Christmas lights illuminated the beautiful building, making it look like something out of a fairy tale.

"No peeping," said Alastair as Isla came out supposedly to greet them, but with a definite glint in her eye as she spotted all the bags and boxes in the boot. Thankfully her bike had been carefully buried under a blanket and all the other gifts so it would remain a surprise until Christmas morning. "You get back inside while we bring all this in. Could you let Mrs Reed know that she can head home now if she likes?"

With one last glance at the boot of the car, Isla returned to the house and Alastair and Isla unloaded the car.

"I'll take her bike and hide it in one of the sheds," said Alastair.

"Good plan."

* * *

Once all the presents were safely hidden away from prying eyes, they heated up the fish pie Mrs Reed had left for supper and steamed some broccoli and carrots to go with it.

Alastair called Isla down.

"Did you have a good day at school?" he asked as she sat down at the kitchen table.

"Yep! And I haven't got any homework because it's almost the end of term."

"I suspect your teachers are looking forward to the holidays as much as you are," Rose said.

"Especially my physics teacher, Mr MacArthur," said Isla, giggling. "His hair is looking more and more crazy!"

"I'm not surprised, dealing with you every day," Alastair teased, "We picked up some end-of-term presents for your poor teachers."

"I'll help you wrap them after dinner if you like," offered Rose. "There are Christmas cards for them all as well."

"Great thank you!" said Isla. "I can't believe tomorrow's the last day of term."

Isla went upstairs to shower once they'd finished eating and Rose and Alastair cleared up.

"Rose . . ."

"Yes . . ." she said, narrowing her eyes at him. It was the way he said her name.

"Did I tell you what a great job you did wrapping all the presents for the staff party last weekend?"

"You did not."

"They looked great," continued Alastair. "Actually, I was wondering . . ."

"If I'd help you wrap your presents?"

"Well . . . yes."

She sighed. "If we do it this evening and if you make me a cup of tea then I will help you."

"I can do better than tea," said Alastair. "How about a mug of mulled wine?"

"That does sound scrummy actually. You've got yourself a deal."

* * *

Alastair went upstairs and returned with three large bags of presents which he put on the floor of the library. He went to warm up the mulled wine while Rose lit the fire and set up three wrapping stations, each with its own tape and scissors. She didn't imagine Isla and Alastair were good at sharing either.

Alastair returned with a plate of Mrs Reed's home-made mince pies and the mulled wine.

"I'll go and get the Alexa from the kitchen," said Alastair. "We can put some Christmas music on and set the mood."

"Must we really?" Rose sighed, mock-exasperated. She actually loved the idea — although was going to protest big time if Noddy Holder sounded out. Working in that Christmas shop really had been a low point. How her life had changed since Alastair had walked in there. She took a moment to appreciate her beautiful surroundings, as well as that she was warm and not wearing a polyester costume.

"Yes!" called Alastair over his shoulder. "I thought all women loved Michael Bublé."

"Not this one!" Rose hollered back. He'd been on repeat in the shop too.

* * *

By the time Isla joined them, Rose had drunk at least half her mug of mulled wine and had twice caught herself tapping her foot along to Michael Bublé's crooning.

Isla's face lit up as she took in the scene before her. She took her place at the table. "This is so Christmassy!" she said, happily, opening up a pack of Christmas cards to write on.

"Do you like the music?" Alastair asked, carefully avoiding looking at Rose.

"It's awesome." Her father gave a satisfied smirk. "It's so awful and cheesy, it's perfect for Christmas."

Alastair's face fell and Rose burst out laughing.

"What's so funny?" Isla asked. "You don't actually *like* this music, do you?"

"Of course not," said Rose, holding her sides. "But it's your dad's favourite."

"Oh my God, Dad! Seriously?"

"It's Christmassy!" Alastair said. "You two have got no musical taste. Alexa, turn the volume up. I need something to drown out these giggling women."

* * *

Isla went to check on Houdini and then watch some television after she'd finished her wrapping and card writing, but Alastair didn't go out to the shed to fetch her bike to wrap until she'd gone up to bed, promising not to come down again unexpectedly.

"She's going to love this," Rose said.

"The amount of wrapping paper we're using on this thing, it's going to cost almost as much as the bike did."

"I did suggest that we just tie a big ribbon on it," reminded Rose.

"But think how much more she's going to enjoy it like this so she can rip the paper off on Christmas morning."

"I agree, but in that case, you need to stop complaining about how much wrapping paper you're having to use!"

Alastair chuckled.

* * *

It was almost midnight when they'd finished and tidied away all the wrapping stuff.

"Shall I put the presents under the tree now?" asked Alastair.

"Is that what you usually do?" asked Rose, absentmindedly.

"We don't usually have a tree," Alastair said after a slight pause, sounding self-conscious.

"Of course, sorry, you did say." Rose still couldn't comprehend why he wouldn't have a Christmas tree for his kid. Even if it was only a little one. "Um, you could, but I'd be

107

worried about the dogs getting at some of the presents, and the bike's a bit obvious . . . Maybe hide them somewhere?"

"Like where?"

"In the wardrobe in my room?" Rose said, in a moment of inspiration. "It's huge. Like a gateway to Narnia huge and I've only put a few things in there."

"Are you sure you don't mind?"

"Not at all, and Isla will never think to look in there."

"Perfect, I'll check she's asleep and then we can take everything up."

Alastair returned a minute later to say that his daughter was out like a light so they crept up the stairs with an armful of presents each.

Rose freed up a hand to turn the doorknob of her bedroom door. She pushed it open with her bottom. It was only at this moment that it occurred to her that it was a little bit weird having Alastair in her bedroom. She did a quick once-over, wishing she'd had the foresight to think of doing so before he'd started walking into the room behind her. Thankfully she'd remembered to make the bed and the place didn't look too much of a state.

She put the gifts on the floor and opened the wardrobe door. "See, plenty of room," she declared, standing back to let him see.

"There is," agreed Alastair. "Let's get everything in there."

"I'll pack them in, you go and get some more of the presents," suggested Rose.

"Good plan. Oh, that's the dress you wore to the Christmas party," he said, pointing out the black cocktail dress hanging in the wardrobe.

"Well remembered," Rose said, knowing she sounded as surprised as she felt. "Well . . . can you bring the bike next so we can pack it at the back in case Isla does happen to come snooping around?"

"On it," said Alastair, saluting with a grin before he left.

A couple more journeys up and down the stairs and all the gifts were safely in the wardrobe.

"Thank you," he said. "This is a good hiding place."

He looked around the room as if he'd only just realised where he was. His eyes rested on the bed for a moment and Rose felt herself blush.

She saw him swallow and he cleared his throat. "Um . . . have you got everything you need in here?"

"Yes, thank you."

"And you like it? Because we can move you to another room if you'd prefer . . ."

"It's lovely," reassured Rose. "Much fancier than my bedroom at home."

"Oh, um . . . good. Well, it's late . . ."

"Yes," agreed Rose. "We should probably be getting to bed . . . to our beds . . . separately . . . to sleep. Oh!" She put her head in her hands.

Alastair laughed – despite his blushes. "You're right, I'm going to go off to sleep in my own bed." He gave her an exaggerated wink before promptly leaving. He left Rose feeling mortified, but she couldn't help laughing too.

CHAPTER 11

"You are absolutely sure you don't mind joining me while I do this?" Alastair asked. It was the following afternoon and they were getting into their respective cars to drive to Isla's school to pick up her and her friends ahead of their end-of-term outing. "I've only just realised that I made an assumption and never really asked you . . ."

"You asked if I was happy to drive your spare Land Rover," clarified Rose.

"True . . ."

"And I think an event organiser should really attend the event," Rose said with a grin. "Plus the burgers sound amazing."

"They are pretty good."

"Also, I want to come," said Rose. "It'll be fun. And, I wouldn't be cruel enough to leave you in charge of six pre-teen girls."

"Thank you, I appreciate that."

They drove to the school and parked up. The girls came over in a group and divided themselves between the two cars.

The girls all wanted to bowl together on one lane.

"Shall we get a lane for us?" Alastair asked Rose.

"I'm pretty good . . ." warned Rose.

"You'll definitely beat me. I'm going to be too busy worrying about who wore the rental shoes last to be able to concentrate on the game."

"Then I'm definitely happy to play you. You book a lane and I'll get the girls drinks. Do you want anything?"

"How bad do you think the coffee is here?"

Rose looked over at the food counter. "I suspect really, really bad."

"I'll have a Coke then."

"Good choice," said Rose, turning to go. "Oh, and Alastair?"

"Yes?"

"Don't book the lane next to Isla and her friends."

"Why not?" Alastair looked perplexed.

"Because," explained Rose, patiently, "look around. There are boys here."

Alastair looked horrified.

"She'll want to look cool in front of her friends. We can keep an eye on them from further away."

"You're right," he finally said with a sigh.

Rose grinned. "I'll be back in a minute with the drinks."

* * *

Alastair truly was terrible at bowling and lost quite spectacularly to Rose, though part of that could have been the fact that he spent most of the three games they played looking over to check no boys were going over to speak to Isla.

"I thought you'd be better at sports," said Rose as they returned their shoes.

"Does bowling count as a sport?" Alastair asked.

"I suppose not," admitted Rose. "But still . . . you were pretty bad." She ignored him as he pretended to look offended. "Right, I'll gather the girls together and we'll head over to the restaurant."

"I'll meet you by the entrance in a minute, I just need to use the loo," said Alastair.

Rose wandered over to the girls, who were removing their shoes and collecting their stuff together.

"Are you having fun?" Rose asked Isla.

"This is the best!" she said. "I got two strikes. Bowling was a great surprise."

"I'm glad you liked it. Are you all ready to eat now?"

"Yep, I'm starving!"

At the restaurant, the group were led over to a table for six, with a balloon floating above it.

"The second table you booked is just over there," the waitress explained, gesturing towards the other side of the restaurant.

Alastair looked like he was going to say something but Rose quickly cut in and said to Isla, "You girls order whatever drinks and mains you like. Don't forget, we're having dessert at home later, though. Your dad and I will be over there." She pointed to the table on the other side of the restaurant where she and Alastair would be eating.

Just the two of them. Like a date, she suddenly realised. How had she not considered that before? Well, there wasn't much she could do about it now.

She took hold of Alastair's arm. "Let's go eat, I'm starving," she said, giving it a little tug.

He reluctantly turned and joined her to follow the waitress over to their table.

They sat down and opened their menus.

"That was sort of sneaky," Alastair said from behind his menu.

"You can still see them and she's having so much fun!"

"She does look happy," admitted Alastair.

"She loves you," said Rose. "But it'll mean a lot to her to have dinner with her friends now."

Alastair sighed. "I guess the company over here isn't completely terrible."

"Thank you," said Rose. "You are so very kind. Now, what do I want to eat . . . ?"

"This is definitely not a place to worry about eating healthily in," said Alastair.

The waitress returned to take their orders.

"A double cheeseburger, fries, onion rings and a strawberry milkshake, please," said Alastair.

"That sounds really good, I'll have the same. Thank you," Rose said.

The waitress took their menus and left.

"I appreciate you being here. I don't feel quite so outnumbered," Alastair admitted, fiddling with a packet of salt.

"I'm having fun," said Rose. "There are definitely far worse jobs. I should know, I've done a fair few of them."

"I'm glad we're not the worst," he chuckled.

"Definitely not. I'd even say I like working for you."

"And we definitely appreciate you being around. It's hard to believe you've been here for less than three weeks. You seem to have fitted right in. I honestly don't know what we'd do without you."

Rose blushed. "Thank you. It's been . . . wonderful being here and helping with everything."

Their milkshakes arrived. "To you, and a Christmas I might actually end up enjoying some of," said Alastair, holding up his drink.

Rose clinked her glass against his, not able to wipe the smile from her face.

* * *

By the time they left the restaurant and loaded everyone into the cars to drive back to the house, Rose's cheeks were aching from grinning and laughing so much. She and Alastair had had so much fun and she somehow managed to work her way through the huge plate of food she'd been served. Rose had been careful to steer clear of certain topics, she didn't want to go into why she'd ended up with the life she had, but they'd talked about their very different childhoods and bonded over school experiences. Alastair had also told her more about how he'd built up his businesses. He'd only checked on his daughter once every minute or so which was honestly better than Rose had expected. The girls were happy and giggly. Rose caught Alastair's eye and smiled.

* * *

Mrs Reed had already left for the night when they returned but the house looked warm and welcoming as they approached with the Christmas trees lit up on either side of the door and all the fairy lights.

They all traipsed in and Isla took her friends to feed Houdini, which everyone was very grateful for as he'd started bleating indignantly from his paddock as soon as he heard the car pull up.

"There's something for each of you on the table in the library," Rose said when Isla and her friends came back into the house.

The girls raced through and found the pamper baskets she'd prepared. Rose smiled at the happy gasps and chatter.

"There's even a basket of treats for Houdini," Isla called out.

"How on earth did you make a pamper basket for a goat?" Alastair whispered.

"Houdini's favourite things are food and being made a fuss of . . . So I just combined the two," said Rose with a shrug. "Mrs Reed said she'd set out the stuff for the ice cream sundaes in the kitchen. I'll just check whether they'd like their desserts now or if they're still too full."

The girls unanimously voted to eat straight away and they took their goodies upstairs to Isla's room while Rose took the ice cream out of the freezer.

Mrs Reed had set out the sundae glasses and spoons on the kitchen island and had made a strawberry sauce and a toffee sauce from scratch after she'd heard that Rose was going to pick up some bottled stuff. There were also various sprinkles, squirty cream, and a large platter of raspberries, blueberries and strawberries to go with the four flavours of ice cream.

The girls helped themselves to the treats and disappeared with them upstairs, much to the consternation of Houdini who bleated by the back door until Alastair gave him some fruit.

"Do you want some ice cream?" Rose asked.

"I'm still full from the restaurant to be honest."

"Me too."

"But I could maybe manage a bit of . . . Chunky Monkey," Alastair said, producing a pot of Rose's favourite ice cream from the back of the freezer.

"How did you know?" she gasped, "And where did you find it?"

"Isla told me and I shopped around."

Rose quickly opened the lid and helped herself to a spoonful. "Oh my goodness, that is *so good*," she said.

"So, not so full after all?" Alastair chuckled as he watched Rose take an ice cream scoop and serve herself a huge bowl.

"Turns out no. Are you gonna join me? Or just watch me eat the whole tub myself?"

"I wouldn't want to get between you and your favourite ice cream . . ."

"I think you need to save me from myself."

Alastair smiled. "In that case . . ."

* * *

They ate their ice cream sitting at the kitchen table and then cleaned up.

"I would go upstairs and work, but I'm guessing you'll tell me that'll spoil Isla's fun."

"I will indeed," said Rose. "You're staying downstairs."

Alastair checked his watch. "There's nearly two hours until that lot are being picked up. What am I supposed to do for nearly two hours?"

"Well, there are some extras left over from the pamper kits. It would be a shame to waste them . . ."

* * *

"You're going to have to get that," Alastair said when the doorbell rang with the first of the parents coming to pick up their daughters. "My mud mask has still got another two minutes to go."

"If this messes up my nails, I will never forgive you," Rose muttered as she got off the kitchen stool.

This was undoubtedly the most fun, if unusual evening she had ever spent, and was ever likely to spend, with a Scottish laird.

CHAPTER 12

The girls were all picked up and Isla went to bed happy and still giggling about her dad giving himself a pedicure.

"Thank you so much for today," Alastair said to Rose as they finished clearing up. "And not just because my feet do feel silky smooth. Isla had a fantastic time. You were right about me staying out of the way."

"Yeah . . ." Their eyes met and Rose felt her cheeks warm as neither of them looked away for several seconds. One of the dogs scratched at the back door, breaking the moment.

"I can't believe she'll be a teenager soon. That's just . . . terrifying," Alastair said, opening the back door for the dog and letting a blast of freezing air in.

"It'll be fine! She's a great kid, and you're a great dad."

"Thank you," said Alastair. "That means an awful lot from you."

"I'd better get to bed. Big day tomorrow."

"Yeah." Alastair sighed and ran his hand through his hair. "It seems like you've got everything sorted for my family descending upon us."

"It'll be a fantastic Christmas," reassured Rose.

"I don't doubt that you'll do a great job . . . I just struggle with this time of year." He gave another sigh and looked at

117

Rose, seeming to be deciding something about her. Apparently she'd passed whatever test it was because he said, "My wife left me on Christmas Eve when Isla was nine months old. She left a note saying that she wasn't cut out to be a wife and mother. She moved back to America where she was from."

Rose put a hand to her mouth. "Oh my goodness . . . that's . . . that's terrible. At Christmas too!"

"Yeah, it does sort of put you off the festive season, to be honest." Alastair's smile was sad.

"Has Isla seen her mother since? She hasn't mentioned her."

"No, I tried to convince Marie to have some contact, but she's refused. I have an address and contact number, but I've got no idea if they still work. The last time I spoke to her was a few months after she left. Unless you count communications through solicitors when we divorced soon afterwards."

"Does she pay child maintenance? Is she in a position to do so?" Rose was surprised at herself for asking this. She half expected Alastair to tell her to mind her own business, but he didn't seem to mind.

"No, my solicitor tried to convince me to push for it, but if she doesn't want anything to do with Isla, then I certainly don't want her money. Also, I have full custody and I want to put myself in the best position in case Marie ever decides she wants Isla to move to the US with her. I can't imagine that happening, honestly, but . . . I guess you never know."

"Wow. I'm so sorry, I can't imagine what that must have been like."

Rose felt the urge to hug Alastair but held back. Would hugging him be completely inappropriate? She really wanted to though.

"So, yeah, anyway, that's why I'm such a Scrooge," he concluded. He let the dog back in.

"You're not a Scrooge," said Rose firmly. She took a deep breath before saying, "My mum passed away last Christmas. She had cancer and she died on Boxing Day."

118

"Oh, Rose, I'm so sorry." And there was the hug. She found herself enveloped in his arms. Her cheek against his strong chest. She felt her eyes pricking with tears.

"Thank you," Rose finally managed to say, looking up at his face. It felt so comforting to be held in his arms. "It was . . . a horrible time. I'd planned to completely ignore Christmas this year, to be honest."

"By working in a Christmas shop?"

"It was the only work I could find at the time," Rose explained as she reluctantly stepped back. She sat down at the table. Alastair joined her wordlessly. "I left my job when Mum found out she was sick, moved back in with her, and became her carer. After she died I was just too broken to go back into organising parties and events for people. I didn't want to be around anyone, actually. But eventually, I had to find some work so I've been doing random jobs for the past several months, waiting until I felt strong enough to decide what I want to do with my life." She fiddled with a gel pen Isla must have left out as she talked.

"I can understand that. I'm guessing you don't have any siblings?"

"No . . . it was always just me and Mum."

"That's tough," Alastair said, gently. "My parents passed away before Isla was born. Car crash. I was just out of university. I was so grateful to have my sister, Fiona, to share my grief with, especially during that first year. I don't know how well I would have managed without her."

"That's so sad," Rose said. "I'm so sorry."

"It was a long time ago."

She sighed. "I really shouldn't be unloading all my woes on you."

"I believe I started it," said Alastair with a smile. "And I'm glad I've told you about Marie. Thank you for trusting me enough to tell me about your mum."

"Christmas can be a really strange time," Rose said.

"Agreed . . . But this is the first year I can remember that I'm not absolutely dreading it, thanks to you."

119

"I'm glad." Rose smiled.

"And Isla is going to have a wonderful time," Alastair reassured her. "She's so excited to have her cousins here. It makes me feel bad for not doing it before, but . . ."

"You couldn't, I get it, they get it. I've got lots of fun stuff planned to keep the kids busy. They're going to have a great time."

CHAPTER 13

Rose woke up the next morning feeling apprehensive. Isla's excitement about her little cousins coming to stay was infectious, but the dynamic of the house was going to change and Rose wasn't sure how she felt about that.

She and Alastair had undoubtedly become closer and she loved spending time with him and Isla. With other people around, would she be relegated and end up feeling more like an employee? Which was fair enough, that's what she was and this was a family gathering, but she'd be sad about it nonetheless.

Rose showered and dressed and decided to head downstairs for breakfast. Isla's bedroom door was still closed; she was probably making the most of being able to lie in. Alastair's was open though.

"Good morning!" said Mrs Reed cheerfully when Rose entered the kitchen.

"You're in a very happy mood," Rose said.

"I love to have a busy house full of people to feed," admitted Mrs Reed. "And it's wonderful to have lots of children around at Christmas."

She passed Rose a full bowl of steaming porridge. "You'd better keep your energy up you've got a full day ahead of you!"

"Yes, I have." Rose laughed. "It should be fun. Do you need a hand with everything?"

"Oh, bless you, dear. I think everything's organised. There'll be chicken casserole for dinner, which I'll get going in the slow cooker in a bit . . . The rooms are all prepared. The boys will be in a room next to their parents, and Aunt Helena will be down the corridor from them . . ."

"You call her Aunt Helena too?"

"Oh yes, I suppose I do." Mrs Reed chuckled. "What time are you picking her up from the train station?"

"Not until three and everyone else is due at five," Rose said. "I've got plenty to do for Saturday night's dinner before then, though. The marquee people will be coming to set up in a bit."

"That sounds like it's going to be wonderful. Right, I must pop out to get some fresh flowers for the bedrooms. I'll see you later."

Mrs Reed left and Rose sipped her coffee and ate her porridge, enjoying the quiet of the morning. The back door opened and Alastair came in. It had been raining and he looked soaked, but very handsome even in a heavy raincoat.

"Hello," he said. "I had to rescue a couple of goats. I had a call they were stuck."

"Lovely day for it," replied Rose, making him smile. "Are they okay?"

"They're fine," he reassured. "Just going to hop in the shower to warm up." He walked past Rose and her nostrils filled with his smell mixed with fresh Scottish air. Rose had to stop herself from letting out a little groan. What was going on with her?

"I've got to head into the office, but I'll be back before you're home with Aunt Helena."

"Great, see you later then," Rose managed to say.

"Oh, and Rose?"

"Yes?"

"Don't let Aunt Helena bully you. She's got a strong personality."

"I'll do my best," said Rose with a gulp.

* * *

Isla asked if she could come with Rose to pick her great-aunt up from the station. Rose was grateful, even more so after Alastair's words that morning. She'd been concerned about how she was going to make polite conversation for the entire journey home with this woman she'd never met before but who was now sounding just a little bit terrifying.

Soon they were driving along the country roads with Isla's music keeping them entertained.

"There she is!" cried Isla as they pulled into the Calton Road pick-up point. She pointed towards a tall woman with long silver hair who was wrapped in what looked like a vintage fur coat. The woman stood next to a much smaller young man in the railway company's uniform, and accompanied by a trolley full of luggage including four large, blank canvases.

"Why does everyone in your family have to be so tall?" muttered Rose.

"Only compared to you," Isla replied, giggling.

Rose pulled over close to Aunt Helena and she and Isla got out of the car to help her with her bags.

Isla was immediately enveloped in a hug by her great-aunt. "My, aren't you beautiful?" Aunt Helena declared. "Are you sure you won't let me paint you?"

"No, Aunt Helena," Isla giggled. "Maybe next time."

Aunt Helena kept an arm around her great-niece but turned her attention to Rose.

"You must be Rose." She looked Rose up and down. "Please call me Aunt Helena, everyone else does."

"It's nice to meet you."

"I'm sure my favourite nephew has been spreading terrible rumours about me," she said with a smile. "Don't believe a word he says."

Rose laughed. "Thank you for warning me."

"This very helpful young man has been assisting me with my luggage," Aunt Helena explained. "If you could just pop the boot open, I'm sure he'll be quite happy to put my bits in there, being especially careful of my art supplies of course."

Rose did her best to hide her smile at the look on the man's face as, under Aunt Helena's close scrutiny, he did as instructed.

"Thank you so much, dear," Aunt Helena said, slipping a ten pound note into his hand which seemed to cheer him up. "You get back into the station now. I'm sure they're missing you."

The young man gave a good-natured grin as he departed. "Will do. Enjoy your trip."

"Would you like to sit in the front, Aunt Helena?" asked Isla politely.

"I shall be quite comfortable in the back, thank you." She opened the car door and elegantly climbed in.

Rose and Isla also got in the car and Rose turned the key in the ignition. Isla's music also came back on.

"What on earth is that racket?" Aunt Helena snapped.

Isla rolled her eyes good-naturedly at Rose as she changed the music to Classic FM. "Sorry, Aunt Helena. I forgot you don't like any music from after the 1800s."

"Cheeky," warned Aunt Helena from the back seat, but she was smiling.

* * *

Aunt Helena and Isla talked about Isla's school for most of the drive back to the house. Aunt Helena did little to hide her disdain for the National Curriculum's art provisions. "I'm hoping you'll come to paint with me at some point over the holiday," Aunt Helena said. "We can try to wipe out some of the dreadful habits you've no doubt picked up since the summer."

"I'm sort of more into maths now," Isla said. "I think I want to be an engineer."

"Artistic skills are of great use to an engineer," huffed Aunt Helena. "And there's absolutely no need for you to choose between mathematics and art at this stage."

"Yes, Aunt Helena."

"So you'll do some painting with me?"

"Of course. You know I love painting with you. Also, Rose can draw really well," Isla said.

"Yes, Alastair mentioned you were an artist," Aunt Helena said to Rose. "Pencil sketching, I believe . . ."

"Oh, not really," said Rose quickly. "I mean, I used to . . . but not very much anymore . . ."

"I would love to discuss your drawing with you at some point," Aunt Helena declared, making Rose's heart sink.

* * *

The basic structure of the marquee was up and the workers had left for the day when they arrived back at the house. Isla and Rose carried Aunt Helena's things up to her room for her, while Aunt Helena had a cup of tea with Mrs Reed. They were an unlikely pair but they seemed very pleased to see one another.

Rose hadn't been into the bedroom Aunt Helena was going to be staying in before.

"This is lovely," she said, as they entered, laden with Aunt Helena's belongings. Huge windows bathed the room in fading afternoon light. The walls were painted an off-white, not at all in keeping with the rest of the house's decor, and there were wooden shutters at the windows as opposed to the thick damask curtains found in most of the other rooms. It made the space seem more modern somehow, almost giving it a Mediterranean feel if you ignored the view outside the window.

"It's the room with the best light in the house, apparently," Isla explained. "Aunt Helena claimed it as her own long before I was born. She grew up here and my bedroom used to be hers."

"Did she also decorate it like this?"

"She *instructed* that it should be decorated like this," Isla clarified. "It gets changed every few years depending on what she's working on at the time. It's been like this for a while now but before this, it was Moroccan themed."

"Moroccan? In the middle of the Scottish countryside?"

"I know." Isla giggled. "But she said Morocco was where her muse was calling her to, so if we wanted her to come and stay she needed it to feel as much like Morocco as possible. She always spends the summer here and she sent Dad an email with Pinterest boards he needed to consult to get it just right before she arrived. He had to put extra heaters in here as well to get it as hot as she wanted. In July."

"That is brilliant," declared Rose.

"Yes, Aunt Helena is awesome," Isla said. "If a tiny bit scary sometimes."

"I trust you two were talking about me," said Aunt Helena, appearing in the doorway and making them both jump. She didn't wait for either of them to reply before she said, "I'm going to have a rest before the hordes arrive." Rose and Isla took that as a hint for them to promptly leave.

CHAPTER 14

Rose returned to party planning in the library until around five o'clock when a car pulled up outside signalling the arrival of Alastair's sister and her family. Rose waited a couple of minutes before going out into the entrance hall to say hello. There were people and dogs everywhere — and Houdini, who'd managed to somehow sneak in all greeting each other. Rose stood to the side, keeping a wary eye on the Christmas tree, intending to defend it from exuberantly wagging dog tails.

"This is Rose," Alastair said, putting a hand gently on the small of her back and drawing her into the group. "She's the reason the house looks so amazing."

"It's lovely to meet you, Rose," said Alastair's sister. "I'm Fiona, and this is my husband, Paul, and the twins are Sam and James."

The boys looked shyly up at Rose who gave them a friendly smile.

Rose could definitely see the family resemblance between Alastair and Fiona, who was tall, dark-haired and striking. Her husband was also tall but had a much slighter build than Alastair. He wore glasses and a suit and seemed like he'd fit more in a city than the country. Rose couldn't help but notice that his sons were two carbon copies of him.

Aunt Helena made her grand entrance down the staircase once the initial excitement was over. She glared at Houdini and gestured to Isla to take him outside. She did so immediately. The twins' eyes widened at the sight of their great-aunt and Rose got the feeling that they were a little nervous of her. She couldn't blame them. Aunt Helena would have terrified her at their age. Frankly, she still did a little.

Mrs Reed came out of the kitchen and was hugged by the new arrivals. "I'll be going in a minute," she said, "but I couldn't leave without seeing you all! My, how you two have grown!" she exclaimed to Ben and James. "Come through to the kitchen, there's a snack ready for you."

The boys and Isla followed Mrs Reed, and Fiona and Paul began taking their luggage upstairs. Rose wasn't quite sure what to do with herself and escaped back into the library to finish packing up work for the day.

It wasn't long before Isla came in with a mince pie for her.

"Oh, thank you, Isla," Rose said.

"I helped Mrs Reed make them earlier. But this is one of hers. Mine are a bit messy and I wanted you to have a good one."

Rose laughed. "Thank you, but I'm sure yours taste just as good."

Alastair poked his head around the door. "Hi there, trouble," he said to Isla, before turning his attention to Rose. "Can I interest you in an alcoholic beverage? We're all going to have a chat in the drawing room until dinner, maybe get some board games out to play with the boys."

"Oh, um . . . I was just going to go up to my room . . ."

"Join us," Alastair said, his gaze earnest. "Please."

"I don't know . . ."

"Please!" begged Isla. "You have got to see my cousins playing snakes and ladders. It's so funny. They try to cheat all the time! You've got to watch them really carefully."

Rose laughed. "Okay then, thank you."

Isla led the way into the drawing room where Paul was opening up a large cocktail cabinet and a drinks fridge. Rose hadn't even realised they were hidden inside the huge mahogany sideboard at the far end of the room.

"Paul is the designated bartender whenever we get together," Fiona explained.

"Dirty martini, sweetheart?" Paul asked his wife.

"Absolutely. Rose, will you have one too?"

"That sounds amazing," Rose said. "Thank you."

"Uncle Paul, will you make me a Shirley Temple, please?" requested Isla.

"Of course, munchkin," he replied.

"I think you're going to need to stop calling me that soon, Uncle Paul," she said. "I'm getting pretty big now."

"You are." Uncle Paul sighed. "But you were such a cute kid, why do you have to grow up?"

"I'm sorry." Isla laughed. "I'm not doing it on purpose."

Isla got down on the floor with her cousins to play some board games and the adults all took a seat. The dogs settled down in their baskets by the fire and the flickering flames cast a warm glow around the room.

Rose sat down at one end of a small sofa and when Alastair returned to the room with some juice for the twins, he took the space next to her. It was an action that made Rose feel hot all of a sudden.

"So, Rose," said Fiona, handing Rose her drink. "How on earth did you end up here organising Christmas for my brother? I'm not even going to start on the fact that if he were a woman he would have sorted it all out himself without even considering hiring someone . . ." She tailed off, giving her brother a pointed look.

"Um . . . well . . . I was working in a Christmas shop and he came in and basically offered me this job within a couple of minutes . . ."

"And you accepted?" Fiona's mouth fell open.

"Well, at the time, I didn't know what a terrible boss he would be . . ." Rose joked.

"What are you saying about me?" Alastair asked, turning his attention from his conversation with his brother-in-law.

129

"You've started going up to random women in London and inviting them to your house," teased Fiona.

Rose saw Alastair shoot a glance at Isla, but she was happily absorbed in playing with her cousins. He glared at Fiona.

"Actually," said Rose, "it was perfect timing. I was looking for another job and I used to work in events management."

Alastair gave her a grateful smile.

"It was lucky that you were able to drop everything and accept his offer then," said Fiona. "And how do you like working here?"

"It's great," Rose replied, truthfully, and happy to be moving on from the subject of how she came to be employed and the fact that she had absolutely nothing to stay in London for. "This house is a dream to decorate and, obviously, Alastair is a brilliant boss."

Fiona nodded. "Well, the house looks amazing. It's so Christmassy! You've got a great eye. We're all very glad you're here."

A victorious squeal indicated that one of the twins had won the tight-fought game of Ludo that had been going on in the corner, and Isla got up to join the grown-ups for a moment while her cousins chose the next game.

"Rose, let me take a picture of you and Dad together," Isla said.

"Um . . . sure," Rose said, not knowing what else to say.

"Can I borrow your phone, Dad?"

Alastair passed his phone to his daughter, somewhat reluctantly it seemed to Rose.

"Sit next to him," Isla said. "A bit closer . . . Dad put your arm around her."

Alastair caught Rose's eyes, checking that was okay. She gave a little nod and felt his arm move around her shoulder and rest there gently. The weight was comfortable and the warmth and smell of him so close made her feel slightly dizzy. How strong did Paul make his drinks?

"Okay! Got it," said Isla. She fiddled with the phone for a moment. "This is my favourite one," she declared, turning it around to show everyone. "Oh my God, you look so good together," she said, returning the phone to her dad.

Rose took a quick glance at the picture and couldn't help giving a little smile which she then swiftly hid. Isla was right; she and Alastair did look good together. And she looked so much healthier than she did a few weeks ago. Her cheeks were pink   probably just due to her proximity to the best-looking man she'd ever met   but her skin also looked clearer and her eyes were bright. Scottish air and Mrs Reed's cooking obviously agreed with her.

She was so caught up in her thoughts that she didn't realise Alastair had left her side.

* * *

They ate in the kitchen, squeezed around the kitchen table as nobody fancied laying up in the dining room. Alastair sat at the other end of the table to Rose and he was kept busy talking to Aunt Helena, while Rose chatted to Fiona, who, it turned out, was an art dealer and had worked for several big auction houses. She'd sold some amazing pieces over the years by artists Rose had admired and studied at university.

The twins were clearly exhausted from their busy day and Fiona and Paul took them for a bath, stories and bed once they'd finished eating. Aunt Helena was determined to see Isla's latest artwork from school, so they went up to Isla's room together. Alastair was left to tidy and Rose automatically started to help.

"You don't have to do that," Alastair said. He appeared very focused on scrapping food scraps into the compost bin.

"I'm happy to help," said Rose. "I'll unload the dishwasher."

"Well . . . thanks, that'd be great."

"Your family are wonderful," Rose said, cheerfully.

"Thank you, I'm quite fond of them," he said a little stiffly.

Rose realised he seemed to be making quite an effort not to meet her eye.

They were silent for a moment before Alastair said, "I need to speak with you about something."

"That sounds serious," Rose said, putting down the tea towel she was holding and turning to face him. "What is it?"

"I'm worried Isla's getting a little too close to you," Alastair said quietly.

"In what way?" asked Rose, carefully.

"Well, you're spending a lot of time together . . ."

"Because we enjoy each other's company and she's been helping me," Rose replied. Alastair took over unloading the dishwasher. He avoided eye contact.

"I'm concerned she's seeing you as a surrogate mother," Alastair explained. "And her photographing us together earlier . . ." He sighed and ran his hand through his hair. "She's never had a mother figure and then, you come along . . ."

"What about Mrs Reed? Or your sister? Surely both of them would count as mother figures, just off the top of my head. They both love her."

"I suppose you're right, but this feels different."

"I can understand your concern," Rose said. "But Isla knows that I'm only here for a few more days."

"She really likes you."

"And I really like her. She's amazing." Rose frowned. "You're worried she's getting too attached to me and will be upset when I leave?"

"Exactly," said Alastair, looking relieved at being understood. "I just don't want her to get hurt."

"Of course not. So, you think it's a better idea for me to keep my distance from this point? To not spend any time with her, even though we both enjoy it?" She couldn't believe what she was hearing. Not only was Alastair being ridiculous but it was hardly practical.

"I didn't say you shouldn't spend any time together . . ."

"Okay," said Rose, warming to her topic. "How much time would be acceptable, do you think? Half an hour a day? Perhaps I could draw up a timesheet to ensure we don't go over by mistake . . ."

132

"Now you're just being ridiculous . . ."

"Am I? Isla and I have been having great fun hanging out with each other. Honestly, it's been good for both of us. And it's going to be difficult for us not to spend time together." Rose had tried really hard to make the run up to Christmas special for Isla and now she felt she was being punished for doing so.

"I don't want her to feel abandoned again," Alastair said quietly. "She adores you. She talks about you all the time . . . It's going to be hard for her."

Rose's annoyance vanished as she felt an ache in her heart for this man and his love for his daughter.

"I understand that," Rose now said, gently. "But it seems a little extreme to stop us spending time together. It's a completely different situation to Marie leaving her. First of all, she's only known me such a short time. Plus, she's always been aware that I'm leaving on Christmas Eve and there's no chance of anything between you and I . . ."

"No chance at all."

"Exactly."

"She knows I don't date," Alastair said firmly.

"Neither do I," retorted Rose.

They glared at each other.

Rose's mouth twitched. Alastair looked so serious and she realised she was actually standing with her hands upon her hips. Alastair's face relaxed and they both started to laugh.

"We seem to be arguing about who dates the least . . ." pointed out Rose.

"I'm sorry," said Alastair, "I'm worrying too much."

"I think so," Rose said. "But thank you for making me aware. I'd hate to hurt Isla. She means the world to me. But she'll be so busy the next few days that I doubt she'll give me much thought, and then . . . well, I'll be back in London."

Rose knew she'd miss Isla terribly. She expected Isla would miss her too, but simply as fun company, nothing like as the mother figure Alastair mentioned. She had other women in her life for that.

Alastair nodded and before he could say anything else, Fiona and Paul came back into the kitchen.

"What were you two laughing about? We could hear you from upstairs!"

"Nothing," said Alastair.

"We were just being silly," added Rose. "Did the boys settle down okay?"

"They both passed out while I was reading to them," said Paul. "They always sleep well when we stay here. Isla tires them out for us."

"The house really does look wonderful, Rose," Fiona said, filling the kettle while Paul took out some mugs. "I can't believe that tree in the hallway. How did Mum and Dad never think of putting one there?"

Alastair shrugged.

"Paul and I fancied a cuppa. Would either of you like one?" Fiona asked.

"I'll have one," Alastair replied.

"I'm fine, thanks," said Rose. "Where did they put the Christmas tree?"

"In the sitting room," said Fiona. "It was just a plastic one but we loved it. We had a fancier one in the drawing room as well but the presents were always put under the one in the sitting room and that's where we'd open our presents on Christmas morning."

"To the sound of that awful Max Bygraves compilation that Mum always insisted on playing," said Alastair with a smile.

"That thing was truly horrendous!" said Fiona.

"It was." Alastair nodded.

"I bet there's still some Christmas stuff up in the attic," Fiona commented.

"I don't think Rose needs any more decorations," Alastair said. "I already feel like I'm living in a Narnian forest."

"They would rather spoil the aesthetic." Fiona chuckled.

"You're more than welcome to have a look up there if you do think of anything you might want to use, though, Rose," said Alastair. "I would have offered before but figured they wouldn't fit the theme you were going for. Our mum never threw anything out."

Isla and Aunt Helena came to join everyone.

"Can we play Monopoly?" Isla asked.

"You can all do what you like," said Aunt Helena. "I'm going to sit by the fire in the sitting room and read my book, ideally with a dog at my feet and a glass of whisky in my hand. I noticed a rather nice one in that drinks cabinet of yours earlier."

"We'll play," said Fiona on behalf of herself and her husband.

"I can take a couple of hours out of my evening to beat you at Monopoly," said Alastair.

"What about you, Rose?" asked Isla. "Please say you'll play too. We can gang up on Dad!"

Rose didn't know what to say. She glanced at Alastair for help and he said, "Of course she will. But don't be so sure that Rose and I won't gang up against you, young lady."

Isla ran off to set up the Monopoly board on the big table in the library. Alastair gave Rose a little smile.

CHAPTER 15

Rose had been told by Alastair in no uncertain terms to take the following day off except for keeping an eye on the continued construction of the marquee. But she had other ideas.

Alastair was going to be in his offices and Fiona and Paul were planning to take the children ice-skating in Edinburgh after hearing how much fun Rose and Alastair had had at the rink. Aunt Helena was travelling with them, but was going to visit an art exhibition near the castle and meet them for lunch afterwards. They'd invited Rose but she'd declined; her bruises from Tuesday were still healing.

Rose's head was full of plans while she sketched in the drawing room after breakfast. It was fun having so many people in the house, but she wasn't used to a big, busy household and she was relishing the quiet. She'd barely been able to hear herself think while she sipped her morning coffee and munched on crumpets with everyone earlier. She couldn't help but compare it to how things would be if she was still in London. She hadn't planned on seeing anyone over Christmas, though she'd sent some cards to friends.

Fiona came in after a little while, the ice-skating party not yet having departed.

"Sorry to disturb you," she said, with a smile. "I'm just gathering everything together and am looking for my book. I think I left it in here . . ."

"Is this it?" Rose asked, handing her a thick paperback which had been on the arm of the chair she was in.

"It is, thank you!"

"No problem," said Rose. She saw Fiona glance down at her sketch-pad and had to refrain from closing it.

"Where did you learn how to do that?" Fiona asked. "I love it."

Rose felt her cheeks turn red. "I went to the Slade School of Fine Art. In London."

"I know where the Slade is," Fiona said, with a laugh. "I would have loved to have studied there, but, alas, I have no artistic talent. I went to UCL and did a degree in History of Art. I had lots of friends from the art school. What did you study?"

"Wow, what a coincidence. I got a master's Fine Art."

"And then . . ."

"And then I had a boyfriend who convinced me that a career in art would be far too volatile and I'd end up starving in a garret somewhere, and so I accepted a job in events management."

"That's a big leap."

"It's something I did during holidays at uni anyway so I knew what I was doing and I got to be creative," Rose continued. "And I didn't hate it, but it definitely wasn't something I wanted to do for the rest of my life."

"So what do you want to do? Now?" asked Fiona, sitting down in the chair next to Rose's.

"In my wildest dreams? I want to be an artist," admitted Rose. "But . . . so few people get to make a living doing that."

Fiona nodded. "It's certainly not the easy option."

Rose sighed. "Anyway, I gave up working on events when my mum got sick so I could look after her. She died last Christmas and I've flitted between rubbish zero-hours, minimum wage jobs ever since."

"Oh, Rose, I'm so sorry," said Fiona.

"Thank you." Rose smiled sadly. "I wasn't able to draw once Mum had gone. She had always supported me and . . . without her . . . it didn't seem right." Rose took a deep breath. "But it feels really good to be spending some time on it again. To be experiencing that flow state where I lose track of time completely, consumed by what I'm creating. I'd begun to think I might never get that back."

"I'm happy for you," Fiona said. "I'm sure your mum would want you to continue with your passion. Especially as you clearly have a talent for it."

Rose wondered whether Fiona was aware of her growing discomfort talking about her mum because Fiona put her hand on Rose's and said, "I'll let you get back to your drawing," and left, presumably to get the ice skaters on the road.

Rose couldn't help feeling a little thrill as she returned to her sketching — did Fiona really think she had talent?

* * *

As soon as the family were all out of the house, Rose put aside her drawing and let Mrs Reed in on her plan.

"I want to go into the attic and see if I can find some of the Christmas things from when Alastair and Fiona were little. The house looks gorgeous, but it's not as they remember it from Christmas and they think there might be some old decorations from their childhood up there."

"I can't imagine they would have been thrown out," confirmed Mrs Reed. "That attic hasn't had a sort through in donkey's years; it's full of all sorts. That's a lovely idea. I can come and help you search now if you like."

Going up into the attic, they were first greeted by all the extra chairs, neatly stacked up, that they'd used for the employee party the weekend before. The space was huge and Rose's heart sank as she wondered how they were ever going to be able to find boxes of Christmas decorations among all

138

this stuff. Thankfully she had Mrs Reed with her who seemed to know the attic like the back of her hand. She walked confidently over to one corner and a moment later held up the top of a Christmas tree triumphantly.

They carried bits of tree and the boxes of ornaments downstairs and put them in the sitting room.

"I didn't decorate in this room because the theme I'd gone for didn't seem to fit it," Rose told Mrs Reed. "It was too fancy for this family space which wasn't going to be used for any events. What I want is to make this room like it was when Alastair and Fiona were little. I thought I could put the tree together and then everyone can decorate it this evening."

"It's a lovely idea."

"Thank you so much for helping me find them. I would have been up there for hours by myself."

"I enjoyed it, and it'll be wonderful to see all the old decorations out again. I'd better get back to work now though," said Mrs Reed.

"Why don't I make you a cuppa to say thank you?" said Rose.

"Now that would be lovely."

Rose made a pot of Mrs Reed's favourite Earl Grey tea for them to share, knowing the housekeeper would approve of her doing things properly, and took her own cup into the sitting room. The dogs followed Rose and immediately lay down in front of the fire which was merrily crackling in the hearth. It made her smile how much they loved their warm spots and how lazy the dogs were in the house.

Rose began by putting the Christmas tree together. It was a decent quality one and, despite its age, looked good by the time she'd fiddled with it and fanned out the branches.

She opened up the other boxes and found strings of fairy lights. She crossed her fingers as she plugged them in to test them and, amazingly, there was only one string of them with a couple of non-working bulbs, which she could just hide behind the back of the tree.

She set to work winding the lights around the tree, making sure they were evenly spaced out. She wanted the family to be able to decorate the tree themselves, but everyone knows there's nothing worse than waiting for the lights to be put on when all you want to do is get started hanging the baubles. She turned the lights on and stood back to admire her work. A little bit of fiddling and she was happy.

Another box was full of tinsel and Christmas card holders which Rose put up around the room. She found a skirt for the Christmas tree in another box along with candles which she placed on the mantelpiece.

She carried anything they'd be able to use for Christmas lunch, like napkins and a tablecloth and table runner, into the dining room.

Another box was full of DVDs of Christmas movies so she moved that close to the television. She pulled out a couple, smiling when she saw *Home Alone*, a firm favourite of hers, and spotted some CDs underneath. Her smile turned to a grin when she saw one of them was the legendary Max Bygraves.

"Would you like some lunch?" Mrs Reed said coming into the room. "Oh, it looks wonderful!"

"Thank you, and I would love lunch. Does everything in here look right? I mean like it used to?"

"There are a few things that are different. The cards used to hang over by the window there, I think."

"Have you got a few minutes to help me get it like it used to be at Christmas?" asked Rose.

"As long as you don't mind just having sandwiches for lunch," said Mrs Reed, smiling as she looked around the room.

Rose left Mrs Reed to work, pleased that she'd accepted her suggestion. She hadn't wanted Mrs Reed to feel that she was being watched as she moved things around to how they used to be placed.

Mrs Reed joined Rose in the kitchen a few minutes later.

"You've done a lovely thing in there," Mrs Reed said, not looking at Rose.

"Is something wrong?" Rose asked, noticing tears forming in Mrs Reed's eyes.

"I'm fine. It was just such a thoughtful thing for you to do and it reminded me of when Mr Duncan and his sister were little and their dear parents were still alive."

"You don't think it will upset anyone, do you?" asked Rose, suddenly worried.

"No, dear. I think it will bring back happy memories," reassured Mrs Reed.

* * *

When Fiona, Paul and the children returned home, they found the sitting room closed and a sign on it instructing: *Do Not Enter.*

"What's going on?" asked Isla.

"Just a little surprise for when your dad gets home," Rose said, mysteriously.

"Can I have a tiny peep now?" Isla begged.

"Nope, not before your dad."

* * *

Poor Alastair was bombarded by his whole family as soon as he stepped in the door.

"Thank goodness you're here!" cried Isla, dramatically.

"Is everything all right?" he asked. "What's happened?"

"Everything's fine," reassured Rose.

"Rose has set up some sort of surprise in the sitting room," Aunt Helena explained. "And we haven't been able to see what it is until you came home."

"Oh," said Alastair. "Can I at least take off my shoes and get changed before we see it?"

"No," said everyone simultaneously.

"Fine." He sighed. "Can we go in there now?" he asked Rose.

"You can," she confirmed with a little nod. "I'll join you in a minute." She suddenly felt embarrassed. What if she'd completely miscalculated and they all hated it? What if it upset people? She hadn't thought this through.

The family rushed out of the hall and towards the sitting room, Alastair glancing over his shoulder at Rose, a quizzical look on his face.

Rose went into the kitchen. Mrs Reed was making hot chocolates for everyone complete with a big bowl of marshmallows, chocolate flakes and cans of squirty cream.

"Aren't you going in with them?" she asked.

Rose shook her head. "I thought I'd give them a minute."

The sound of running feet soon reached them though and Isla came bursting into the kitchen followed by the twins. "Oh my goodness, Rose, it's amazing! Dad says you have to come and join us!"

Rose laughed. "I'm glad you liked it. Help me carry these things and I'll come through."

"Hot chocolate!" exclaimed James.

"You have to drink hot chocolate while you're decorating the Christmas tree," explained Rose. "Mrs Reed, you'll come as well, won't you?"

"Of course I will," she said, removing her apron.

The twins ran back to the sitting room armed with the marshmallows and squirty cream and Rose, Mrs Reed and Isla followed them rather more sedately with the drinks.

"This is just wonderful, Rose," said Fiona, accepting a hot chocolate. "Thank you so much! It's exactly like how Mum used to decorate it."

"Mrs Reed was a great help," said Rose.

"You're a wonder, Mrs Reed," said Fiona, surprising the housekeeper with a hug.

"Oh, it was nothing," Mrs Reed said, looking flustered. "It's nice to see the old treasures being used again."

"Are you lot going to start decorating that tree then?" said Rose, noticing the twins impatient glances at the boxes of decorations.

"Absolutely," said Fiona. "Kids, you get stuck in. I'm going to enjoy my hot chocolate and watch you do all the work."

"One final thing," said Rose, picking up the Blu-ray player remote. She pressed play and Max Bygraves began to play.

"Oh my goodness!" said Fiona, turning to her brother. Alastair put his arm around her and gave her a squeeze.

"I'd hoped that CD had been destroyed years ago," muttered Aunt Helena from the armchair she'd made herself comfortable in.

"Don't be such a grump, Auntie," said Fiona. "It's traditional."

Rose looked at Alastair; he'd been conspicuous in his silence. His eyes met hers and she felt heat fill her body. She held out the tray she was carrying and he accepted a drink. "Thank you," he said quietly. "For the tree and . . ."

"You need marshmallows in that, Uncle Alastair!" said James, interrupting the moment and causing Alastair to break eye contact as he bent down to allow his nephew to add marshmallows to his drink.

* * *

"It looks brilliant," declared Isla, standing back to admire the tree.

"It does," agreed Mrs Reed.

"I love my own tree and the fancy one in the entrance hall as well," Isla said, "They're beautiful, but this is a proper family tree."

"I agree," said Fiona, hugging her niece.

"What have we got for the top?" asked Isla, looking around.

"Here," said Mrs Reed. "Will this do?" She handed Isla a glittery star.

"It's a bit small . . ." said Isla.

"We just used to put random things on there when we were little," Fiona said. "Your dad was so cross one year because your granny let me put my Malibu Barbie on top and he thought it looked stupid."

"I remember that," said Alastair, with a grin. "And I maintain that it did look stupid."

Fiona stuck her tongue out at her brother making the children laugh.

"What did you have on your Christmas tree when you were little?" Isla asked Rose.

"We had a fairy," Rose said. "She was absolutely beautiful, with a china face, golden hair and delicate silver wings. She used to belong to my grandma who was given her when she was a child. My mum was always so worried she'd get broken and I had to be so careful when I put her on the tree and when we packed her away again after Christmas."

"Do you still have her?" asked Fiona.

"No," Rose said, with a sad smile. "She was lost. My mum got sick and had to move into a hospice and, somehow, our fairy got misplaced when the Christmas tree I'd brought in to decorate her room was taken down and packed away."

"Oh no," said Isla.

"We're so sorry about your mum," Fiona said.

"Thank you," said Rose. "It was . . . a pretty terrible time, but back to this glorious tree! What are we going to do about the top?"

"Let's put the star on there for now and maybe we can think of something better later," suggested Paul.

"You okay with that, guys?" Isla asked her cousins and when they nodded in agreement, Isla placed the star proudly on top of the tree.

It had taken the children an hour to make sure every decoration was in exactly the right spot while the adults exclaimed over forgotten treasures like the bauble with a Christmas pig on that Alastair had made at school when he was about six.

Mrs Reed happily stayed until the last bauble was placed. "What a lovely start to my Christmas break," she said as she was preparing to leave with the twins hanging off her.

"You've been an absolute breath of fresh air around her," she whispered to Rose as she hugged her goodbye.

Rose fought back tears. If it was this hard saying farewell to Mrs Reed, how much worse was it going to be with Isla? Her mind went to never seeing Alastair again and she quickly focused on going to get Mrs Reed's present. She hoped she liked the watch she and Alastair had taken an age choosing for her in Edinburgh.

After Mrs Reed left, it was decided that Rose and Alastair would finish up making supper while Fiona and Paul took the twins upstairs for an early bath and Aunt Helena and Isla started a jigsaw puzzle together in the library.

Once everyone else had left the sitting room, leaving Rose and Alastair collecting up empty mugs, Alastair put his hand on Rose's as she was about to walk out of the room with a full tray.

"Thank you," he said. "This was so thoughtful and it means a lot."

"I'm glad you like it," she said with a smile.

"I love it. I can't believe I'm saying this, but thanks to you, I think I'm actually kind of looking forward to Christmas."

"That's brilliant," Rose said, though the thought of Christmas itself and the fact that she would be by herself and hundreds of miles away from this house and the people in it made her feel suddenly sad. At least she was helping towards making this family's Christmas a good one. She tried to cover her sadness with a grin before Alastair noticed her mood.

Alastair still had his hand on hers. She looked down at it and he quickly moved his hand away. "Let's get this food cooked so we can start a Christmas film before it gets too late for the twins," Rose said, cheerfully. Her hand now felt cold and somehow lacking.

CHAPTER 16

When Rose woke up the next morning she was still smiling, remembering the lovely evening she'd spent with Alastair and his family the day before.

Everyone had agreed that the choice of movie should be down to her, so she decided on *The Polar Express*, a favourite of hers made even more special now she'd watched the twins experience the magic of it for the first time.

She was so busy going over the wonderful time she'd had that it took a couple of minutes before she remembered that today was the day of the Christmas party for all Alastair's business associates — the big party that absolutely had to go perfectly, and all the contractors she'd employed to decorate and put the final touches to the marquee would be at the house in under an hour she realised checking the time on her phone.

Rose got up and headed straight to the bathroom for a shower. Even the fact that the water wasn't quite as hot as she'd like couldn't put her in a bad mood this morning. There was something charming about the house's old plumbing being more than a little temperamental.

She layered up her clothes. It was going to be a cold day and she crossed her fingers that the marquee was going to

146

be warm enough. The marquee company had assured her it would be nice and toasty so she just had to trust them, she supposed, but that aspect of the preparations was probably what was worrying her the most. Closely followed by the toilets not working or people getting food poisoning . . .

Isla was having her breakfast in the kitchen when Rose came downstairs.

"Where's everyone else?" Rose asked, putting the kettle on.

"Aunt Helena will still be asleep as she's hardly ever up before ten. The twins woke up early so Aunt Fiona and Uncle Paul took them out with the dogs for a walk. And I think Dad has gone for a run."

As if he knew he was being spoken about, Alastair came through the back door kitted out in that running gear of his.

"Good morning," he said cheerfully.

"Morning, Dad." Isla didn't move her eyes from the back of the cereal packet she was reading.

"Good morning," said Rose. "Mrs Reed said she's hung your suit for tonight up in your wardrobe."

"Great, thanks. What time are all the suppliers coming to get things set up?"

"In about twenty minutes," Rose said.

"I shall make myself scarce then," he said, making Rose smile at the thought of how much he hated people in and around his house.

The day seemed to pass by in a blur as soon as the contractors started work. Rose had made sure that as little as possible would be happening inside the house, which led to a lot of time spent outside talking to the workers.

Isla was fascinated by what was going on and was happy to be kept busy bringing drinks and snacks out to everyone. Naturally, Houdini also wanted in on the fun which led to some mayhem and stolen biscuits before it was agreed that he had to be on a lead if he came round the front of the house.

By 3 p.m. the florist had finished work decorating the tables with gorgeous centrepieces. The lights were also done and the marquee was as toasty-warm as the company had promised. The caterers had arrived and were busy cooking and the swing band Rose had managed to book thanks to a cancelled wedding would be arriving soon. Rose had tried to feel sorry for the couple involved, but she was very glad she'd been able to get hold of some live music.

She was on her way inside the house to get a cup of tea when Alastair came out of the front door. "Just the woman I was looking for!" he said.

Rose smiled. "What can I do for you?"

"We've had a couple of people drop out for tonight and I was wondering if you'd like to take one of the places? I know you're working but everything looks like it's coming together really well and you'll still be on site and available if anyone needs you. Plus this way you get to eat the food, which smells delicious by the way."

"Oh, um . . ."

"It seems a shame to let the food go to waste," wheedled Alastair.

"No, it's really nice of you, and I'd love to," explained Rose. "It's just that I haven't got anything to wear for it. I didn't bring anything black tie worthy with me . . ."

"I don't mind what you wear to it . . ."

"But I do," insisted Rose. "I was going to change into a black shirt and trousers tonight so I'd just blend into the background."

"You could never just blend into the background, Rose." Alastair's cheeks flushed and their gazes locked. He cleared his throat. "Um . . . could you maybe borrow something from Fiona?"

"Fiona's almost a foot taller than me," said Rose, laughing. "I doubt she'd have anything that would fit me."

"Okay, well it was worth a try. If you change your mind, there's a spot for you."

"Thanks. I appreciate the invite."

She watched Alastair go back inside. She so wished she was accompanying him tonight . . .

* * *

Rose checked her watch. It was almost 6 p.m. and everything was going according to plan. The marquee people had left, and the serving staff were setting the tables inside the marquee. The band had arrived and was setting up on the stage which had been erected for them and guests were due in an hour for the five-course dinner, followed by dancing.

It was a good time for her to go inside and get changed into her uniform for the evening. She let everyone know where she'd be and was about to head to her room when a white car drove up the driveway and stopped outside the house. Had a guest got the wrong time and arrived early? Rose didn't think anyone else was due. What would she do if they had? she wondered quickly. Could someone entertain them in the drawing room until the other guests turned up?

The car door opened and a woman in a beautifully cut shift dress stepped out. She looked lovely but she wasn't dressed for a black-tie event, so Rose didn't think she could be a guest.

Rose walked over to the car to greet her.

"Hi, can I help you?" she asked the woman.

"I've got a delivery for . . . Rose?" the woman replied, checking a piece of paper in her hand.

"That's me," said Rose, puzzled.

"Oh, great!" The woman opened the back door of the car, pulled out a garment carrier and handed it to Rose. "This is for you then."

"Are you . . . sure?"

"I'm sure!" said the woman getting back in the driver's seat. "It needs to be returned by Tuesday." She started the car and drove back down the driveway.

Rose took the garment carrier upstairs to her bedroom. She lay it on the bed and slowly opened it. Inside was a pale blue full-length dress and another bag containing a pair of low-heeled court shoes. The dress was strapless and the skirt was made up of layer upon layer of thin layers of fabric. It was beautiful. Rose stared at it, both puzzled and delighted, and held it up in front of her.

There was a knock on the door.

"Come in!" Rose called without taking her eyes off the dress.

"Hi," said Fiona as she came into the room. "Do you like it?"

"You ordered this for me?" Rose asked.

"No, my brother did, but he asked me to check the size and that he hadn't chosen something completely horrible. He really wants you to come tonight," Fiona said with a smile on her face.

Rose didn't know what to say.

"Do you like it?" Fiona repeated.

"Of course, it's beautiful," said Rose, "But . . ."

"Don't overthink it," said Fiona. "It would be a shame for the food to go to waste and it looks and sounds like you've organised an amazing night. You should be part of it."

"But the point is that because I'm in charge of everything running smoothly tonight, I need to oversee it."

"You still can. You'll be right there."

"I guess . . ."

"Why don't you try on the dress and decide then?" Fiona suggested, very cunningly Rose thought.

Rose raised an eyebrow. "You know that if this fits, I'm not going to want to take it off."

Fiona winked. "We'll see. I'm going to get dressed myself. Paul's giving the boys their dinner. It must be so nice to be a guy and take five minutes to get ready for something like this . . ."

Fiona left and Rose unzipped the dress and stepped into it. She breathed a sigh of relief when she realised it fitted.

The dress was pleasantly heavy, making her feel like Scarlett O'Hara. She looked at herself in the wardrobe's full-length mirror. She had never worn anything like this before, and most likely never would again. How had Alastair even managed to hire it at such short notice?

It was so thoughtful of him. It must have cost a lot to hire something like this, and it would be rude of her not to wear it . . . And it would be a lot of fun to join in the party. And, yes, being that much closer to Alastair during the night was a large part of the appeal. She wasn't going to even attempt to deny that.

She sat down at the dressing table and began to apply some make-up, wishing she'd thought to do it before trying the dress on as now she was worried she'd get something on the fabric. She supposed she could just take it off but she couldn't bear to somehow.

She'd just finished when there was another knock on the door, "It's me again," said Fiona. "Can I come in?"

"Yes," called out Rose.

Fiona entered, wearing a full-length black dress with a slit up the side. Her smoky eye make-up and slick up-do completed the look.

"You look amazing! How did you manage to get ready so quickly?"

"Practice," replied Fiona with a laugh. "I wondered if you'd like a hand with your hair."

"I really should be getting back outside . . ."

"Don't worry, Aunt Helena is reading to the twins and I sent Paul down a few minutes ago to check that everything was running smoothly and he says it's all fine. It will only take me a few minutes to do your hair . . ."

"Okay then, thank you," said Rose.

* * *

When Rose walked down the stairs, clipboard with her to-do list in one hand and holding her dress up with the other, she couldn't help feeling self-conscious. Her hand kept creeping up to check on the messy chignon Fiona had put her hair in. She wasn't used to being this fancy.

The huge marquee was divided in two so that there was an eating and bar area and a dance floor. The plan was for guests to be welcomed into the bar area to mingle and then find their seats in the dining area when the caterers and waiting staff were ready to serve the first course. The marquee company had done a fantastic job, it was lovely and warm and looked great with white fairy lights and lanterns illuminating the space and crisp linen and sparkling glasses on the tables.

"Rose. You look amazing," came Alastair's voice from behind her.

She turned and looked up at him, so tall and handsome in his dinner jacket, and smiled as she picked up the subtle clues she now knew meant that he was uncomfortable and would much rather be in the house preparing to spend an evening playing board games with his daughter than being polite and making business chat.

"You don't scrub up so badly yourself," she said. The grin she received in return made her tummy flip. "Thank you so much for the dress, it's beautiful," she managed to say, focusing on the list in her hands. "And you knew my dress and my shoe size."

"Thanks to Isla and Fiona. And it's nothing," said Alastair. "You've done a fantastic job and I'm glad you can be at the party."

"Me too."

"You do realise that this dress is the same colour as the one I wore as Elsa in the Christmas shop?"

Alastair blushed. "I knew the colour suited you," he mumbled, before changing the subject by commenting, "This all seems very under control."

"Fingers crossed!" she said.

"You don't need luck."

"Hi, Dad, hi Rose! What do you think?" Isla ran over to join them. She wore a silver, knee-length dress with spaghetti

152

straps which Rose had helped her to choose and she looked lovely. She was thrilled that she was allowed to attend until supper was served and then was going to head into the house. Thankfully Aunt Helena thought there was nothing worse than spending an evening with a load of business people and had offered to stay in the house and spend the evening with Isla, keeping an ear out in case the twins woke up.

"You look lovely," said Alastair to his daughter, giving her a kiss on the head.

"Aunt Fiona did my hair," she said, turning round to show them the part up-do her aunt had done for her.

"She did a great job," said Rose. "She did mine too."

"And you look fantastic, Rose!" said Isla. "Like a duchess or something."

"Thank you, sweetheart." Rose tried not to blush as she felt Alastair's eyes on her again.

A car drove up the driveway and the hired parking attendant went into action, showing the driver the area that had been set aside for parking.

"I guess the show's about to begin," said Rose. "Let's get into position."

* * *

As the evening progressed, Rose realised she was really enjoying herself even though she was very much in work mode. Everyone was dressed in their finest, with several of the men in kilts. It all felt very glamorous.

Guests had arrived to a welcoming glass of champagne or freshly squeezed orange juice, and then mingled, enjoying their drinks and company while canapés were brought around and classical music played gently in the background. When it was time for the first course to be served, Rose observed the waiting staff help everyone to find their seats.

As luck would have it, Rose was at the same table as Fiona and Paul enjoying a child-free night. Sarah, Lucy's mum, had been seated at the table furthest from Alastair thanks to a little bit of strategic planning on Rose's part.

Rose kept looking around to make sure everyone attending seemed happy and that nothing appeared to be going awry with the event. She checked that Alastair was all right; he sat on a table with his most important business contacts and didn't seem too pained at making polite conversation. Keeping half an eye on Sarah, Rose observed how she spent most of her time watching Alastair. She certainly didn't seem very interested in anyone she was seated with.

The swing band set up as the panna cotta dessert was served and it began playing as people finished their coffees. Rose had been worried that no one would want to dance, but she couldn't have been more wrong. As soon as the band started playing, people got up and made their way through to the dance floor.

Some of the people from Alastair's table had gotten up to dance, but Alastair remained seated, talking to a man and a woman.

Rose went around the marquee, checking in with the staff to ensure things were running smoothly before heading outside to the catering vans to see that everything was good there as well. The December night air was freezing and Rose returned to the marquee as quickly as she could.

She stood watching the band, absentmindedly tapping a foot to the music and enjoying the feeling of warming up now that she was back inside.

"Would you like to dance?" She turned and found Alastair standing next to her, holding out a hand.

"I'm supposed to be working and I don't want my boss to think I'm slacking off," she replied, acutely aware of how close he was.

"Don't worry." He took her hand in his. "I'll let you know if I see him coming."

Rose allowed herself to be led onto the dance floor and before she could worry about it being awkward to dance with him, Alastair spun her around and she couldn't help but laugh. She could feel Alastair relax as they danced and they grinned at each other. The rest of the world seemed to fall away until it was just them and the music.

The song finished and they stopped, still holding hands, caught in a private world. Then Rose felt a tap on her shoulder. It was one of the caterers.

"Hi, Rose, we're all done."

"Oh, brilliant." She let go of Alastair's hands. "Let me come outside and thank everyone." She smiled at Alastair. "Thank you for the dance."

"My pleasure."

She turned to go.

"Wait," said Alastair. "Take this." He took off his jacket and placed it round her shoulders. "It's cold out there."

"Thanks," she said, so incredibly touched by the gesture. She held his gaze for a moment longer, before turning to follow the caterers.

* * *

As the caterers drove off, Rose stood for a moment staring up at the stars with Alastair's jacket wrapped tightly around her. He didn't wear aftershave, but the smell of presumably his shampoo and well, him, made her smile. However, although his jacket did help, it was nowhere near warm enough to keep out the cold. She headed back into the marquee, anxious to return to Alastair.

But when she entered the space, he wasn't back at his table. Glancing around she caught sight of him on the dance floor. Laughing and dancing with Sarah. Her arms were wrapped around his neck as they moved together.

Rose's stomach sank and she felt tears pricking her eyes. She quickly turned away, blinking furiously, and almost bumped into Fiona.

"Oh! Hi, Rose!" Fiona said. "Are you all right?"

"I'm fine!" Rose's voice was a little too high.

Fiona looked over Rose's shoulder. "Oh," she said.

Fiona opened her mouth to say something more, but Rose interrupted her. "Alastair very kindly lent me his jacket. Would you be able to give it back to him for me? I really must check on the bar staff." She handed Fiona her brother's jacket.

"I'm sure he's just being polite," Fiona said, quietly.

Rose waved her hand. "Whatever. As long as everyone's enjoying the evening." Rose walked quickly over to the bar area where she tried to make herself look as busy as possible.

CHAPTER 17

Rose still felt out of sorts the following morning. She stayed in her room until the desperation for coffee drove her downstairs. She was glad to get away from the dress; draped on the chair in front of her dressing table it appeared to be judging her for her behaviour the night before.

It was Christmas Eve tomorrow and she was going to be leaving. Instead of making the most of her remaining time here, she'd gone and behaved ridiculously. She'd spent the hours until the last of the guests left doing her absolute best to avoid Alastair at all cost. All she'd actually succeeded in doing was spoiling her own enjoyment of the evening and making everything awkward and horrible for herself. Hopefully not for others . . . She winced as she remembered Fiona's take on things.

Alastair had only danced once with Sarah and then returned to his table, where Rose, hidden behind a balloon display, watched him glance around the room — was he looking for her? — before he put on his dinner jacket. He'd stayed there for a while and then moved around the other tables for the rest of the night, the consummate businessman. Rose had seen Sarah approach him a couple of times, but they hadn't talked for long and Alastair remained off the dance floor for the rest of the evening.

Rose danced a few times with Fiona as Paul steadfastly refused to set foot on the dance floor, but she always kept a watchful eye to make sure Alastair wasn't coming over. Fiona and Paul were fun and good company, but it wasn't the same as when she'd danced with Alastair. She caught Alastair looking at her several times as the evening went on, but pretended not to notice.

"Are you really going to ignore my brother all night?" Fiona had asked, when Rose spotted Alastair coming over to them and promptly declared she needed the loo.

"I'm not ignoring him!" Rose insisted, unconvincingly. Fiona rolled her eyes as Rose swiftly walked in the opposite direction to Alastair.

Now in the cold light of day, Rose couldn't believe she'd behaved so childishly. So, she had a bit of a crush on her boss . . . She was an adult and she should be able to control herself. It's not like she actually wanted anything to happen between them anyway. The last thing she needed while she was trying to get her life back on track was a man complicating things. And he'd made it completely clear that he didn't date. Though it appeared Sarah hadn't received that memo. What possible difference did it make to Rose who he danced with? It must have been the alcohol she told herself firmly. Except she'd stuck to sparkling water all night because she'd been working.

The kitchen was empty. Rose made herself a strong coffee and stuck some toast on. She guessed everyone had taken the dogs and Houdini out for a walk. It was still a few hours before they were due to go for the treat she'd booked — she, Alastair and Isla were taking the twins to see Father Christmas at a local farm shop. The shop was kitted out with a kids indoor play area so sounded perfect for a pair of six-year-olds. Paul was going to take Fiona out for a spa afternoon which was part of her Christmas present from him.

Rose was not looking forward to facing Alastair but at least with the children there'd be plenty of alternative focus and they wouldn't be alone together. Not that she should have a problem being alone with him, for goodness' sake . . .

Almost as if she'd conjured him up, Alastair walked into the kitchen with the dogs.

"Good morning," he said.

"Good morning." She wished the ground would open up and swallow her whole.

"You did a wonderful job last night," he said, brightly. "Everyone had a brilliant time. I'd definitely use the caterers and the band again."

"I'm so glad." Rose, focused intently on her coffee.

"Did you enjoy yourself?" Alastair continued.

"Of course."

"Good . . . because I was worried I'd done something to upset you. You gave Fiona my jacket and then seemed to be avoiding me . . ." He put a tea bag into a mug and reboiled the kettle.

"You were just busy so giving it to Fiona seemed . . ."

"But I wasn't . . . busy," Alastair said quietly.

"My mistake," said Rose as lightly as she could.

"Okay . . . that's good, then. Good . . . As everyone else is out, I wondered if you had time to help me with something?"

"Sure . . ." What else could she say?

"There's something we used to do when I was a kid at Christmas. It was kind of a family tradition, and I think I'd like to revive it."

"Okay . . ."

"My dad and I used to head out together to get a yule log. The biggest log we could find that would fit into the fireplace on Christmas Eve. We'd always get it a few days early so that it dried out a bit in front of the fire before Christmas Eve." He poured water into his mug, added milk and put the tea bag in the food compost bin as he talked.

"That's such a cool idea!" Rose couldn't help forgetting her awkwardness at this Christmas tradition.

"We used to light the fire after dinner on Christmas Eve and put the yule log on it. Fiona and I would sleep downstairs, or rather lie awake downstairs watching the fire and the Christmas tree and waiting to see if I could catch Father Christmas coming down the chimney. The idea was that the log would burn all night. I honestly can't remember if it ever did."

"What a lovely tradition. It shall have to be added to the official Christmas activity itinerary."

"I'd agree, expect Isla wasn't interested in coming. She suggested you might like to though . . . So, do you want to come out now and help me find the yule log?" he asked.

"Of course," Rose found herself saying. So much for keeping out of his way . . . "Who else is coming?"

"Just us," Alastair said with a shrug. "Everyone else has gone out for a while to do some last-minute shopping. Except Aunt Helena, but I doubt she's even up yet."

"Are you sure Fiona won't want to do it with you?" asked Rose, feeling mildly panicked. *Just the two of them?*

"I thought it would be a nice surprise for her, and going to get it was always something I did with Dad. She'd be making mince pies with Mum and Mrs Reed."

"Okay, sounds fun. I can be ready in five minutes."

Rose hurried upstairs to her room and got bundled up, once again thankful for the loan of Isla's wellies which now lived on the boot stand in the hallway so she could use them whenever she needed.

When she came back downstairs, Alastair was waiting by the door with a small chainsaw in hand.

"You look ready to massacre," Rose joked.

Alastair grinned. "We're going to get the biggest piece of wood we can find that will fit into that fireplace."

"You've taken exact measurements, right?" Rose teased.

Alastair looked at her incredulously. "Do you honestly think I haven't had those measurements memorised since I was eight?" he asked.

Rose laughed. "You're really taking this seriously, aren't you?"

"If you're going to do something, you may as well do it properly."

"Fair enough. Let's head out with that chainsaw of yours then . . ."

* * *

They set out on the same route Isla took Rose on. There was no uncertainty this time; she trusted Alastair and was confident he knew exactly where he was going. She was grateful that he didn't lead her uphill though, rather taking them along fairly level ground and into a woodland.

They followed a path winding through the trees. Rose did her best to dodge the worst of the mud.

"Growing up, this place was like a playground for Fiona and I," Alastair said.

"It sounds like you had a wonderful childhood," said Rose.

"Yes, I did. What about you?"

"It was just me and Mum, but it was good. Very different to yours, but I was happy and loved."

"I'm glad," he said, looking over at her. "It's important you've got those memories."

"It is. It's comforting to have them."

They wandered around, pointing out potential candidates for this year's yule log. Any that looked particularly promising were checked with the measuring tape Alastair had in his pocket.

"I've asked Aunt Helena to move in," Alastair said, offering his hand to Rose as she stepped over a fallen tree trunk.

"Oh, wow. What did she say?"

"She said she'd think about it," Alastair said with a wry smile. "She hates the idea of being dependent on anyone but I know she's struggling by herself. Fiona's asked her before and she said no, but Aunt Helena hates Manchester and she thinks Fiona will fuss over her."

"And you won't?"

"I'll try not to," Alastair said with a laugh.

"Do you think she'll say yes eventually?"

"I don't know," he said. "I've offered her her room in the house permanently, which is what I'd prefer, or she could have a cottage on the estate so at least Isla and I would be close by if she needed us." He was quiet for a moment. "She had a heart attack in June," he continued, quietly. "Only a small one, and the doctors say she's doing well now . . . but . . ."

"You're worried about her," Rose finished for him.

"Yes," he admitted. "And I'd like her close by so I can help if she needs it."

"That sounds like a really sensible idea," said Rose.

The sky got darker and darker, and Rose glancing up at it anxiously. "Um . . . we might want to hurry, it looks like it's going to rain soon."

"Finding the perfect yule log cannot be rushed," murmured Alastair as he measured yet another piece of wood.

"We're supposed to be looking after the twins in just over an hour and Aunt Helena can't take over if we're not there because she's painting all morning and threatened to throw things at anyone who disturbed her," reminded Rose.

"You make a good point." And at that very point the heavens opened.

"Oh, great," Rose said on a sigh. "Please tell me that's the log we're going to take home."

"It might be . . . But we've got at least four centimetres to spare. I think we can do better."

Twenty minutes later, Rose was completely soaked through and would have gladly abandoned Alastair to his fate if she'd been absolutely sure of the way back to the house.

The mud was so thick in places that walking was slow and difficult and she was thoroughly fed up with this whole stupid tradition.

"That one looks fine," she snapped, as Alastair measured yet another log that looked exactly the same as about twenty of the others he'd measured.

Alastair stood up decisively. "I want to re-measure that one by the big oak . . ." And he wandered back the way they'd come.

Rose swore under her breath as she felt more rain going down the back of her neck. "Please, can we go back now?" she asked.

"Bear with me, let me just check this."

Rose was getting wetter and wetter and increasingly grumpy. She could be sketching in the nice dry sitting room right now, enjoying the warmth from the fire, but no, she had to agree to go on this ridiculous quest. She narrowed her eyes at Alastair's back.

"Ah ha," Alastair said happily, seemingly unfazed by the pouring rain and Rose's animosity. "This is the one! We'd better start heading back. Don't want to be late for Fiona and Paul."

He picked up the log.

"Could you carry the chainsaw for me?" he asked cheerfully. "Turns out we didn't need it after all."

Rose glared at him. The only thing that could have made this whole stupid experience worse was having to carry that stupid chainsaw, and there you go . . .

"Or . . . I can just carry it . . ." said Alastair. He popped its carrying strap over his shoulder.

"I think that's probably a better idea."

"It'll be quicker for us to get back if we continue on and do a circuit," said Alastair, striding down the path.

Trying to focus on being back in the dry, Rose followed him.

They came to a little stream, with some large rocks forming a path across it. Alastair stepped on one confidently, barely changing his walking pace. Rose, however, slowed down, searching to see if there was a better place to cross; the rocks were very wet and slippery. Alastair hadn't realised she'd stopped and was marching on ahead. She neither wanted to lose sight of him nor have to call him back to help her. She decided just to go for it and hopped onto the largest, closest of the rocks . . . She immediately discovered that Isla's old wellington boots didn't have the greatest grip in the world. Her foot slipped and almost before she knew what was happening, she'd yelped, there was a splash and she found herself sitting in the middle of the stream with a sore, wet bottom.

Alastair turned and ran back to her, dropping the log and his chainsaw.

"Are you all right?" he asked, stepping on one of the stones to get closer to her. He took her hand and pulled her out of the water.

"No, I'm not all right!" Rose cried, indignantly. She looked down at herself. She was a mess.

"I mean are you *hurt*?" Alastair said. Rose glared at him as she spotted a twitch at the corner of his mouth.

"My bum hurts," she said. "But I'm okay, I think."

"Can you walk?" Alastair prompted. "Or do you need me to carry you back?"

"And leave your precious log?" snapped Rose.

"I would leave my precious log if you needed me to." Alastair spoke so gallantly that a little laugh almost escaped from Rose despite the situation.

"I can walk," she said quietly. "I can't believe this. The bruises have barely healed from ice skating."

"We'll take it slowly." Alastair picked up his things.

They walked back to the house in silence apart from the squelching of water and mud coming from inside Rose's boots. Alastair went to put the chainsaw back in the tool shed while Rose took her boots off outside the back door and trudged up the stairs to have a quick bath before the children returned. Though it would serve Alastair right if he had to take them to see Father Christmas by himself . . . If she hadn't solemnly promised Isla she'd be there, she'd be very tempted to leave him to it.

She was absolutely freezing and shivering as she sank into the hot water and closed her eyes. What a disaster of a Christmas activity. Why would Alastair even want to do something like that? It was awful! *Because it was something he used to do with his dad when he was small . . .* said a little voice in her head.

He missed his dad and he really struggled with Christmas and had asked her to do one little thing for him. He'd gone from not wanting to have anything to do with Christmas to trying to get into the Christmas spirit and trusting her enough to want to include her in restarting a family tradition he loved. And she'd gone and got in a strop because of a little bit of mud and rain. Okay, the dunking in the stream was unfortunate, but, big picture, she should have behaved better. *Again!*

She forced herself out of the warmth of the water and wrapped herself in a towel.

She got dressed and went downstairs. She found Alastair in the kitchen.

"I made you a cup of tea," he said, holding out a mug.

"Thank you," Rose said, accepting the drink and sitting down at the island. Alastair took the stool next to her.

"Are you all right?" he asked at the exact same time she said, "I'm sorry."

"You answer my question first," Alastair urged, with a smile.

"I'm fine." She shook her head at herself. "But I shouldn't have got as annoyed as I did. You asked me to join you, and it was important to you and . . . well . . . I was a bit rubbish. It was only a bit of mud and rain. There was no need for me to make such a fuss or to be so grumpy."

Alastair let out a deep laugh. "Are you kidding me? You made it perfect!"

"What?" asked Rose incredulously.

"Every year when I was little, my dad and I would go out together to get my *precious* log." Alastair looked at her with raised brows when he said precious. "It felt like every year we got rained on, and Dad got annoyed with me for taking too long choosing, and then we'd end up arguing over which was the best log . . . By the time we got home we were usually barely speaking to each other." He laughed out loud. "Then my mum would act as peacemaker, making sure we got warmed up and feeding us, and all would be forgiven."

"This sounds like a truly terrible family tradition now that I hear all the details," declared Rose.

"I'm sorry you had a bad time and that you fell over in the stream."

"I appreciate you managing not to laugh at me when that happened."

"I was worried about you. Though once I knew you were okay, you looked so mad, I didn't dare laugh."

"I was pretty mad," agreed Rose. "And my bum hurt. Why do activities I do with you tend to end up with me sore?"

Alastair grinned which, for some reason, made Rose blush. "Hopefully seeing Father Christmas later will be pain-free."

"It had better be," muttered Rose, taking a sip of her tea.

"I've put the log in front of the fire in the sitting room to dry out, by the way . . . Would you like to see it?"

"I don't want to hear another word about that stupid log," Rose snapped, but she was smiling.

"Fair enough. May I make you a peace offering slice of quiche and some salad for lunch before everyone gets back?"

"I would love some lunch, but you don't need to make a peace offering, we're good," Rose reassured him.

"Well, if there's anything I can do to make up for the terrible time you had earlier, I will gladly do it," Alastair said sincerely.

"I may hold you to that," Rose threatened.

Rose checked her phone while Alastair put lunch together. She had a missed call from a local number. As she was about to ring it back, her mobile rang again with the same number showing.

"Hello?" she said, accepting the call.

"Hello, this is Tina from the Cairn Farm Centre. I'm calling about our Father Christmas experience. I believe that you have tickets booked."

"That's right," said Rose. "At three o'clock."

"I'm very sorry, but our Father Christmas has been taken ill. We're trying to find someone willing to take his place for this afternoon, but we haven't had any luck so far."

Without missing a beat, Rose asked, "Would he need to supply his own costume?" Alastair glanced over at her with raised eyebrows.

"Oh no, we have a variety of sizes of costume here. We just need someone before three this afternoon."

"I think I may have just solved your problem." Rose grinned at Alastair. "Your replacement Father Christmas will be with you by two thirty."

* * *

"I cannot believe you're making me do this!" Alastair said, yet again, as Rose helped him on with the Father Christmas costume in a store room at the back of the farm shop.

"Imagine how upset the twins would have been if their Father Christmas visit had been cancelled!" Rose said. "You know how much they've been looking forward to it. And Isla's been really excited about bringing them here."

"I'm pretty sure they could have found someone else to step in," grumbled Alastair.

"They hadn't been able to and it's only for a few hours," Rose said. "Anyway, I think this beard kind of suits you." She gave his big white beard a gentle tug.

She stepped back to take in the full effect. "Very believable," she said, before whipping her phone out and taking a few photos before Alastair could stop her.

"Right, I'd better get back to Isla and the twins. The longer I'm here, the more likely they'll do something to upset Aunt Helena," Rose said. "Have fun! Oh, and on the subject of costumes, don't forget about returning the dress you hired for me. You were going to do that today?"

"It's on the back seat of my car. I'll make a detour on the way home."

Rose was heading to the door when she stopped. "Are you sure you don't mind? This, I mean? The Father Christmas thing?"

"Not at all," Alastair said on a dramatic sigh. "You'll have all the kids, after all. This is easier!" Thankfully he was smiling.

"Okay." Rose went to leave again, but turned back. "Thank you, by the way. So much. For getting me the dress. I've never worn anything like it before and I felt like a movie star or something."

"You looked beautiful in it," Alastair said softly, catching and holding her gaze.

Rose's heart skipped a beat. She forced a light-hearted response. "Thank you, Santa," she said, before fleeing to find Aunt Helena and the children.

* * *

Rose was giggling to herself at the thought of Alastair in his costume as she met up with Isla and the twins; they were in the indoor play area being watched over by a rather unimpressed-looking Aunt Helena.

"Thanks for keeping an eye on them," Rose said on joining her.

"I wouldn't miss my nephew doing this for the world, but I do wish there weren't quite so many children around."

"It is a Father Christmas experience," Rose pointed out. "It's not completely unusual for there to be children here."

"Well, I don't see any need for them to be quite so loud," Aunt Helena said huffily.

Rose signalled to Isla to come and join them.

"I can't believe Dad's going to do this," Isla whispered to Rose.

"Me neither," Rose confessed.

"Do you think James and Sam will recognise him?"

"I guess we'll find out soon," said Rose.

They walked across the store and outside to the barn where Santa's Grotto was set up and an elf checked tickets. 'Santa Claus Is Comin' to Town' was playing, bringing back painful memories of that song being stuck on repeat for hours when she worked in the Christmas shop.

They joined the short queue.

"Do you think we'll get a present?" James asked Rose, looking up at her with wide eyes.

"Oh, I'd imagine so," she said. "I bet you've both been very good boys this year."

The look that passed between the twins at this point was probably the cutest thing Rose had ever seen.

"You know," she said, "Father Christmas doesn't expect you to be perfectly behaved all the time."

"Really?" checked James.

"Really," Rose confirmed.

"Are you all going to come in with us?" Sam asked.

"Oh yes," said Rose.

"Even you, Aunt Helena?" asked James.

"I don't want to miss this," Aunt Helena replied.

"It's a shame Uncle Alastair couldn't come," said Sam.

"It is, but I'll make sure I take lots of photos for him and your mum and dad."

They were close to the front of the queue so it didn't take long for it to be their turn to go in.

The elf showed them all through the door into a large room. There was a pretend fire at the far end and a large red armchair in which Alastair sat resplendent as Father Christmas, wicker baskets full of wrapped presents on the ground next to him. There was a much smaller armchair next to him for a child to sit in and share their Christmas list with him.

"Ho ho ho," said Alastair in a suitably deep Father Christmassy voice. "Which one of you is going to come to speak to me first then?"

Rose glanced over at Isla who stood between her and Aunt Helena. They shared a sneaky grin at Alastair's surprisingly good performance.

The twins had already discussed this at length and several rounds of rock, paper, scissors later had come to the agreement that James would go first.

"I am!" James cried excitedly.

Rose saw Alistair fiddle with his beard to ensure that as much of his face was covered as possible and began taking photos on her phone. Fiona would definitely want to see this and Rose knew she wanted to capture it for herself as well.

"Well, why don't you come and sit down next to me and you can tell me what you'd like for Christmas?"

James sat on the edge of the chair. He was clearly very nervous. Rose smiled at him to try to reassure.

"What's your name then, young man?" Alastair asked.

"James," came out as a squeak.

"And have you been a good boy, James?" asked Alastair. Rose caught his eye; she suspected he was enjoying himself.

"I think so," said James, carefully.

He was so nervous he wasn't able to look at Father Christmas.

"I happen to have been told that you have been very good," Father Christmas reassured him. James looked slightly happier.

"And what would you like for Christmas?" Alastair asked gently. Rose spotted him giving Isla a wink and heard his daughter stifle a giggle.

James looked stricken. In all the excitement it seemed he'd completely forgotten what he wanted to ask for. Rose didn't know what to do. The two boys had been discussing what they'd ask for in the car on the way there. Should she interfere? Would that embarrass James?

Suddenly Sam piped up with, "He'd like a football goal and gloves, please."

James looked at his brother gratefully.

"And what's your name?" Father Christmas asked.

"I'm Sam. I'm James's twin brother. I'm actually twelve minutes older than him."

"Would you like your brother to come and join us?" Father Christmas asked James. James nodded and Sam marched forward, his brother wiggling over in the armchair to make room for him.

Alastair looked up and caught Rose's eye. She smiled in response as Sam started explaining the exact football he'd like and how he and his brother were going to start their own football team.

* * *

Alastair gave Rose a wink as the boys chose a present each and trailed out of the grotto with Rose, Isla and Aunt Helena.

"Shall we get back to Uncle Alastair's house so we'll be there when your mum and dad get back?" Rose said.

"Yes," said Sam, excitedly. "I want to play with Houdini!"

"You can give him his tea if you like," offered Isla. "Both of you can do it," she added quickly, seeing James's face fall.

"Wasn't Dad brilliant?" Isla said once her cousins were out of earshot.

"He really was," agreed Rose.

"I don't think the twins had any idea who it was."

"He was very convincing!"

"Thanks for everything you've done by the way, Rose," Isla said quietly. "I just know this is going to be the best Christmas ever."

"I hope you're right . . . I'm a bit nervous."

"I'm most definitely right, and there's absolutely no need for you to be nervous. Even Dad is looking forward to it and he can't stand Christmas usually."

"I'm sure that's not the case," said Rose, diplomatically.

"It is. He tries to pretend he's having fun, but I know he's glad when Christmas is over. But not this year."

"I'm so glad," said Rose, smiling.

"You know," said Isla slowly. "It's not his fault my dad's kind of grumpy about Christmas . . ."

Rose put an arm around her. "He told me about your mum." Rose felt it best to be honest.

"Cool," said Isla. She let out a little sigh and looked relieved. "I'm glad you know."

"I'm sorry about what happened."

"Thank you," said Isla, her eyes focusing on the ground. "I don't remember my mum and I've got lots of people who love me."

"You and your dad make an excellent team."

"We do. I love having you here too though. You're really fun." She stopped and hugged Rose tightly.

"I've loved being here too," said Rose, refusing to allow herself to think about her return to London tomorrow.

They approached the car and Rose opened the doors for everyone.

"Isla, will you go in the back with your cousins, please," called Aunt Helena.

"She just doesn't want to be stuck in between the twins talking about football," Isla whispered to Rose, giggling. "Of course, Aunt Helena," she replied at a normal volume.

Had she truly managed to change how Alastair felt about Christmas, Rose wondered. Now she knew about Isla's mother, she completely understood why Alastair had spent so many years avoiding Christmas as much as possible, but it must be lovely for Isla to see her dad joining in and enjoying the festivities. She certainly couldn't have imagined the Alastair she'd met a few weeks ago dressing up as Father Christmas and winking at her!

* * *

The children entertained themselves with Houdini and the dogs and cartoons until their parents came home. Rose waited until the boys and Isla had gone back into the sitting room before showing their mum and dad the photos from the grotto. Father Christmas himself wasn't due back for another couple of hours.

"It looks like my older brother actually made a half-decent Santa Claus," said Fiona, laughing. "Thank you so much for organising this for the boys. It really meant a lot to them."

"I'm glad they had a good time, and it was certainly more enjoyable than the other Christmas tradition I got roped into today. Yule logs are more trouble than they're worth."

"Yes," said Fiona, rolling her eyes. "I always thought that was a daft idea, hence why I chose to never partake in that particular piece of festive fun. Especially with the arguments that invariably ensued!"

Rose winced. "You and your mum had the right idea," she said. Though she knew that if Alastair asked her to go out with him again now, in the dark, to get another perfect log, she'd be pulling on Isla's still soggy old wellies and heading out there with him. But she wouldn't get the chance to do anything like that again because it was almost time for her to leave and return to her little flat in London.

If her visit to Scotland had taught her anything, it was that she'd reached the point where she needed to step out of herself a little bit and open up to other people again. She didn't want to be alone grieving in her home anymore. Her mum would want her to start properly living life again, and that included prioritising her art.

Hopefully, this would be the last Christmas that she spent by herself.

She'd decided not to make a big deal about leaving; it seemed silly to as she was just there to do a job. Would she even be missed when there were so many people here all happy to be enjoying Christmas together?

Feeling a little maudlin, Rose excused herself and went up to her room so she could recalibrate and get control of her feelings before joining everyone for her last dinner in the house. They were all so happy and excited about it being Christmas Eve tomorrow. It wouldn't be right for her to bring them down with her melancholy mood.

She lay down on her bed, going over all the preparations and everything she'd put in place for Alastair's family's Christmas. She was so pleased with how everything had gone so far, but also very aware of how soon it was until she was leaving and that she wouldn't get to experience many of the fruits of her labours. She shook her head; this wouldn't do. She should start packing, distract herself.

She'd brought and wrapped presents for everyone. She knew they wouldn't be expecting it, but she'd wanted to. As a tiny thank you for what they'd done for her. Without them, who knows how long she'd have carried on in London living her half-life. Now she'd started drawing again, she knew how important it was for her to continue and work towards a career that somehow had art at its centre.

She heard the dogs bark and Houdini bleating as Alastair came home, and decided she'd just give herself a few more minutes and then she'd go down to join everyone. Finally, she forced herself up off the bed. It would soon be time for the dinner Fiona had been preparing to be served.

There was a knock on her bedroom door.

"Rose?" said Isla's voice.

"Come in," she called out and Isla opened the door, popping her head around it comically and making Rose smile.

"Hi, sweetie," Rose said.

"Aunt Fiona's wondering if you have got a minute? We wanted to talk to you about something in the kitchen."

"Sure." Rose hoped a last-minute problem hadn't raised its ugly head.

She followed Isla down the stairs and into the kitchen where she was surprised to see the whole family gathered, even the twins looking very serious sitting on the stools at the kitchen island and working their way through a plate of Mrs Reed's sugar cookies. Her gaze went straight to Alastair, who was making everyone hot drinks in the corner.

"Is everything all right?" Rose asked, looking around at all the people gathered there.

"Everything's fine," said Aunt Helena firmly. "But there's a problem with the Christmas preparations."

"Oh no, did I forget to do something?" Rose asked. "Is it too late for me to correct whatever it is?"

"No, no, don't worry. I'm sure you've arranged everything for us perfectly," said Fiona. "We've just come to the conclusion that there's something we need, in order to make this Christmas extra special and we didn't realise right away."

174

"We really hope you can help us with it." Isla was smiling.

"What is it?" asked Rose, praying it was something she could fix before she left.

Fiona elbowed her brother who had stayed quiet in the corner.

"We were . . . um . . . hoping you might consider staying here for Christmas with us," he said, meeting Rose's gaze and holding it for so long that Rose began to feel rather warm.

Fiona rolled her eyes at her brother, and continued explaining, "Please don't feel in any way pressured to stay. It's just that you said you didn't have plans for the holidays and we'd love to have you here."

"We don't want you to go," added Isla, earnestly.

"You've put so much work into making sure we have a great time, it would be a travesty if you didn't get to experience the fun as well," said Paul.

"And if you stay, you can have my pantomime ticket and I can get out of an afternoon of torture," said Aunt Helena, making everybody laugh.

"Oh, wow," said Rose, overwhelmed and suddenly feeling tears prick at the corner of her eyes. "I don't know what to say . . ."

"Say yes!" cried Isla. "It'll be so much fun to have you here!"

Rose looked around at all the people in the room, all eager to hear her decision. Would it be awkward for her to essentially gatecrash this family's Christmas? If someone had asked her just a few weeks ago, she would have said she'd never do something for that. And yet . . . somehow staying over Christmas didn't seem like such a ridiculous idea . . . she was here already and it wasn't like she had anything she needed to get back to London for. She hadn't thought she'd be bothered about Christmas and had planned to spend it like any other day, doing her best not to fall into reminiscing about the Christmases of the past, spent with her mum.

Staying here certainly seemed appealing. It would be lovely to be with people and to see the children opening up the presents she'd helped to choose . . .

Of course, she did need to sort herself out with a job as soon as possible, but how much would she be able to do over Christmas anyway? She'd just be sitting in her flat by herself trying to ignore the fact that everyone else was having a good time with friends and family. What was the point in doing that when she had people here wanting her to stay and enjoy Christmas with them? A Christmas she knew would be wonderful because she'd carefully planned it to be!

But what about Alastair? What about him? she demanded of herself. She seemed to have developed something of a crush on him, but she'd get over it. She'd probably never see him again after Christmas. She mentally shook her head. That didn't need to be dealt with right now.

"If I am going to stay then I think I need to earn my keep," Rose said with a little smile.

"What? No, don't be ridiculous," Alastair said, aghast. "I want you here as a guest . . ."

"Well, I'm afraid I must insist on organising one final event: a little cocktail party for Christmas Eve. We'll set up a bar in the library again."

"Can I be in charge of mixing the drinks?" Paul asked, a twinkle in his eye.

"Of course," said Rose.

"Can I come?" Isla asked.

"Certainly," replied Rose.

"Can we come?" asked Sam, his arm round his brother.

"You can come at the beginning but then you two are going to have to head to bed so that you can go to sleep and Father Christmas can deliver your presents," said Fiona. This agreement seemed to satisfy the twins.

"Can we play jazz music and pretend we're in the basement of a New York jazz club?" asked Aunt Helena.

"Naturally."

"Can Houdini come?" asked Isla.

"No, I'm afraid not," said Rose. Isla gave a little shrug; it had been worth a try.

176

"As everyone appears to be in accord, I suppose I can agree to your terms and conditions," concluded Alastair.

"Oh, those aren't all my terms and conditions," said Rose.

"Should I be worried?"

"We need to cook a proper Christmas lunch," Rose explained. "Roast turkey with all the trimmings. I'm not eating a takeaway like you'd planned to on Christmas Day."

"Seconded," said Fiona.

Alastair turned his attention to his sister. "You said a takeaway would be fun!"

"I knew Mrs Reed wasn't going to be around and I didn't want you to get stressed cooking a huge meal for everyone . . . Especially knowing how you used to feel about Christmas. I was trying to be accommodating."

Alastair smiled at Rose and nodded decisively. "Fine, we will all cook Christmas lunch together. We can go out tomorrow to buy the ingredients."

"Excellent. Let's eat now then," said Fiona. "We can hash out the rest of the details before the boys go to bed."

Rose caught Alastair looking at her and grinned. She realised she was now properly excited for Christmas. Something she honestly hadn't thought was possible.

CHAPTER 18

Rose and Alastair set off to the supermarket early the next morning, hoping that it might mean that they missed the worst of the Christmas Eve crowds. No one else had wanted to go with them, citing that it was Alastair's fault for not getting the food in before, and Rose's for making it a proviso of her staying that they have a turkey. They all seemed to have conveniently forgotten that they were just as keen on having a proper Christmas dinner as Rose.

"You realise this is going to be a nightmare, don't you?" Alastair said, pulling into the busy car park.

"It'll be fine," reassured Rose. "We're completely organised, we have our list and our shopping bags."

"It's going to take hours . . ."

"No, it won't," said Rose, grabbing a trolley. "We'll be done in no time."

"Rose . . ." Alastair said, stopping her gently. "Can I check something with you?"

"Sure, what is it?"

"You weren't bullied into staying with us, were you? I mean my family can be a lot when they set their mind on something and I know that this was going to be a difficult

178

Christmas for you. If you want to go home, I'll deal with them and take you to the train station."

"I want to stay," said Rose, holding his gaze. "It was lovely to be asked by everyone. I was dreading Christmas, and it's still going to be hard, but I think it'll be much easier surrounded by you all." She had almost said that it would be easier with him, but managed to stop herself just in time. "I'm actually looking forward to Christmas now."

"Me too," said Alastair. He stared into her eyes a little longer before pulling away and saying, "This evening should be a lot of fun."

"And the twins will be so cute opening their presents tomorrow."

"They will be. I hope Isla likes her bike."

"She's going to be thrilled with it," said Rose.

They walked into the supermarket. By the entrance there were piles of chocolate tubs. Alastair picked up two. "Heroes or Celebrations?" he asked.

"Um . . . Heroes, definitely," said Rose. "Bounties are the worst chocolate bar ever invented and what is even the point of a Milky Way?"

"Exactly!" said Alastair. He put the tub of Heroes in the trolley. They walked around the supermarket, bickering cheerfully over food choices and picking up what they needed. It was busy but everyone seemed to be in the festive mood and the staff were quickly restocking the shelves so they managed to get everything they needed, including an enormous turkey.

* * *

They got home with pasties for an early lunch which they picked up from a bakery on the way back. The twins were so excited at the thought of Father Christmas coming, they didn't seem to quite know what to do with themselves.

"I think maybe stopping the sugar for a while might be a good idea," Fiona suggested, with both twins under the kitchen table attempting to have a lightsaber fight around the dogs.

"Have you got more wrapping to do?" asked Alastair.

"Yes, Paul and I got some done earlier, but there's still more. Have you?"

"Nope, Rose got me all sorted with that."

"I hope you didn't get her to do all your wrapping for you?" Fiona said sternly.

"No, unfortunately, she made me do it." He caught Rose's glare. "Fine, she helped me with it," he admitted. "Anyway, it's dry out at the moment, would you like me to take the boys out for a walk? Burn some of their energy off."

"That would be amazing," said Paul, wincing as he got booped on the knee by a lightsaber.

"Not a problem," said Alastair. "Hey guys, do you want to climb up to the hill fort with me?" he asked the twins, who roared their approval.

"Isla, will you come?"

"Sure!" she replied.

"Rose, you're not going to leave me to handle this lot all by myself, are you?"

"I hate that hill," admitted Rose. "It's torturous!"

"Please come, Rose!" said Isla. "It will be so much fun if you're with us."

"You can use a dog to pull you up it," Alastair suggested.

"Okay," said Rose. "But I reserve the right to be grumpy."

"You be as grumpy as you like." Alastair chuckled. "Aunt Helena, what about you?"

"There is no way on earth you'd convince me to go up that ridiculous hill," Aunt Helena stated, "so don't even try. I shall sit and read in the sitting room by the tree, enjoying some peace and quiet." She looked pointedly at the twins.

Fiona took this as her cue to quickly round up her children. "Let's get you two ready, shall we? You'll need to be well wrapped up to tackle that hill!" She ushered them out of the kitchen.

* * *

The hill climbing party returned a couple of hours later with two well-walked and much calmer little boys in their midst. The twins combined with the animals were so distracting that Rose found going up the hill much easier this time. She might even have enjoyed being out in the fresh air for a while.

Fiona and Paul were still locked away in the library getting the last of their wrapping done, so Alastair helped the twins out of their muddy outdoor clothes while Rose made the three children hot chocolates, making sure to use the Transformers mugs Alastair kept especially for the twins. She took them through to the sitting room, where even Aunt Helena was smiling at how cute the twins looked sitting on the sofa on either side of their bigger cousin as Alastair put on *Arthur Christmas* for them.

"Rose," said Aunt Helena. "I was wondering if you'd be able to help me with something upstairs for a little while."

"Um . . . of course." Rose guessed she needed a hand with some wrapping or carrying presents down.

She followed Aunt Helena up to her room where an easel was set up with the canvas Aunt Helena was currently working on.

"May I?" Rose asked.

"Of course," Aunt Helena said and Rose went over to the canvas to take a closer look. It was a watercolour of a city scene, but what really stood out was the people milling around, so vibrant going about their everyday lives. Aunt Helena's style was almost Impressionist as she managed to convey so much character with seemingly few brushstrokes and defining details.

"Edinburgh?" Rose guessed.

"Yes, I began sketching for it in October when I had an exhibition there."

"I love the light falling on this section," said Rose.

Aunt Helena nodded.

"What did you need me for?" Rose asked, not taking her eyes off the painting. She felt like she could study it for hours.

"I would like you to join me while we have the last of the evening light," Aunt Helena said simply. "This room has a wonderful view and I'll bet you haven't had a chance to begin capturing it yet. I've set up the table for you by the window."

Rose walked over to the table. Fresh paper and a new box of sketching pencils lay enticingly upon it.

"Thank you, but I don't draw . . ."

"I've spoken to Fiona and Isla about you," Aunt Helena said. "And I'm interested to know if what they say is true. You have begun drawing again I understand and you may as well do it here as anywhere else. And if you're anything like me, I imagine you could do with a break from the noise of downstairs."

Rose considered arguing, but she realised she didn't want to. Aunt Helena seemed to be sure the discussion was finished anyway and went over to her easel where she carefully put a large men's shirt on over her clothes and picked up a paintbrush. Rose sat down at her table and opened the box of pencils, taking a moment to close her eyes and inhale their delicious scent. She selected a 3B, and began to draw.

* * *

The women worked in comfortable silence. Aunt Helena was right, the room did have the best light in the house.

Rose was so engrossed in her drawing and in getting as much down on paper as possible before the sun set, that she hadn't realised Aunt Helena had stopped work and was standing behind her until she gently said, "That is quite lovely."

"I'm very rusty," Rose confessed.

"Fiona was right," Aunt Helena commented before moving back to her own easel. "Do you work in any other medium?"

"Watercolours, actually," admitted Rose.

"But you haven't felt the urge to paint while you've been here?"

"Actually, I have. Some of the views are spectacular, but I didn't bring paints or watercolour paper with me. I hadn't done any form of art for so long. I don't even know why I brought my sketchbook and pencils to be honest . . ."

"I would be very interested to see you paint. You've lost the light now, but perhaps you'd like to join me here again? And you are more than welcome to use my paints."

"I would love that," Rose found herself saying. It was heartfelt. She was rewarded with a smile.

* * *

Rose came downstairs from her drawing session feeling almost trance-like.

"You look like you had a good time," said Alastair, coming out of the library.

"I did," said Rose, with a grin. "Your aunt is . . ."

"A force to be reckoned with," Alastair finished for her, making Rose laugh.

"And a great artist and teacher."

"She is," agreed Alastair.

"What have you been doing?" Rose asked, attempting to bring herself to the present moment.

"I've been starting to get things ready for this cocktail party you're insisting we have," Alastair teased.

"Would you like some help?"

"Absolutely."

"Let's take a look at what we're working with then . . ."

"Great, oh, and I invited Mrs Reed and her family. They'll be here at eight."

"Excellent, we need everything looking perfect for her."

"Yes, boss." Alastair indicated for her to go into the library first.

All the wrapping stuff had been packed away so that the library could be transformed into a New York basement jazz bar as requested and Alastair had started moving tables around and bringing in more chairs. The table lamps dotted around, provided perfect lighting.

They were soon joined by Fiona and Paul who began setting up the bar area.

Alastair disappeared to much grumbling from Fiona who was certain her brother was just hiding away eating chocolate somewhere to get out of work.

However, when Alastair returned, he was carrying a vintage record player.

"Oh, wow!" said Fiona. "I remember that! Where did you find it?"

"I thought I recalled it being in the attic, and I struck lucky. There are also a couple of boxes of records up there. If one of you wants to give this a clean and set it up, I'll go through the records and find any that sound jazzy."

"That is an excellent idea," said Rose. "I'll wipe it down for you."

"Thanks," Alastair said, handing her the player. Their fingers touched and his gaze lingered just a little too long making Rose's cheeks warm and her insides fizzle before he left again.

* * *

Rather than cooking, they ordered vast quantities of Chinese food for an early dinner.

"So takeaway is fine at Christmas as long as it's not actually on Christmas Day?" Alastair said, sarcastically as everyone tore into the containers.

"Yep," said Rose, taking a bite of a spring roll. "But don't you agree that it's going to be much more fun to cook a big meal together tomorrow?"

"I do," said Alastair. "I'm happy to admit that I was wrong and that I'm looking forward to a proper Christmas dinner. As long as I'm not in charge of making sure the turkey's cooked. I don't want anyone poisoned."

"Yeah," said Fiona, "That's definitely a job for someone else."

She had a prawn cracker thrown at her in retaliation, much to the delight of her children.

* * *

When they'd finished eating, Paul and Fiona took their very excited boys upstairs to bath and get into their pyjamas while everyone else cleaned up, apart from Aunt Helena, who excused herself early declaring she needed longer to prepare for the cocktail party than the young people. Of course, no one minded one bit, and Rose noticed the concerned look Alastair gave his aunt, checking she was all right and wasn't overdoing things.

Everyone else soon went to get ready for their fancy evening. Rose didn't really have much choice on what to wear; it would have to be her black cocktail dress again. But that didn't matter. She felt nice in it and it was kind of perfect for the occasion. She did her make-up and put her hair up in a sleek bun. When she gave herself a final check in the mirror, something was missing . . . She added some red lipstick. It wasn't a shade she'd usually wear and she wasn't even sure why she'd packed it, but she liked it. The thought briefly crossed her mind that she hoped Alastair would like it too.

* * *

When she came downstairs, the twins were on the sofa being read *The Night Before Christmas* by Isla while Fiona and Paul sat on the other sofa watching. It was just about the cutest thing Rose had ever seen. She surreptitiously managed to get a couple of photos to send to Fiona later.

She slipped out of the room, not wanting to intrude on this family time and almost collided with Alastair.

"Oh, sorry," she said, and glanced up to meet his eyes.

"You look . . . great," he said, his gaze moving down her body and back up to rest on her lips, making her blush.

185

"Thank you. So do you." And he did, he'd changed into a fitted grey suit which he wore with a crisp white shirt with the top two buttons undone, showing just a hint of chest hair. But Rose knew that she liked him best when he was wearing his old jeans, which she happened to notice hugged his bottom very nicely, and one of his thick wool jumpers. But she could also appreciate him like this, especially as he looked significantly more relaxed than when he was usually wearing a shirt.

"Did you spot my precious log on the fire?" he asked, smirking.

"I'll be glad when that stupid thing is nothing but ash," replied Rose, making Alastair laugh.

"Would you like to help me choose the music for tonight?" he asked with a raised brow. "I brought down a load of records and I need to whittle them down. Oh, and check that the record player still works of course."

"I'm happy to do that," said Rose with a smile.

"You," said Alastair, "are an absolute star, thank you."

"Not a problem, all part of the service," joked Rose.

"You're not on a clock now," Alastair said, suddenly serious. "I hope you're here because you want to be with us . . . with me."

"Uncle Alastair!" called Sam running into the room and breaking the moment, "Mum can't find any carrots for Rudolph!"

"I guess story time's over then," said Alastair, giving Rose a smile before turning his attention completely to his little nephew, "Don't worry, buddy. I know where they are. Why don't you help me choose a good one?"

* * *

An hour later, the boys were in bed and the cocktails were flowing. Mrs Reed had seemed pleased to see Rose still in the house and hugged her warmly when she and her husband arrived. She'd now moved on to one of Paul's lethal margaritas.

The record player that did work! was proving to be a huge success and there were many good-tempered arguments about whose turn it was to choose the next song.

"Rose, I would like to speak with you for a moment, if I may." Aunt Helena tapped Rose on the shoulder.

"Of course. Are you having a good evening?"

"Just wonderful, dear. And I really cannot begin to describe the difference you have made to this home. You truly have brought the spirit of Christmas here."

"Thank you." Rose was touched, "That's such a lovely thing for you to say."

"Well, it's the truth! But that isn't actually what I want to talk to you about now," continued Aunt Helena, purposefully. "The fact of the matter is that I have a job offer for you, young lady."

"A job offer?" repeated Rose.

"Indeed. I'm guessing my nephew has told you that he's invited me to live with him?"

"He has," admitted Rose.

"Well, I plan to take him up on his very kind offer. It's time for me to accept that I'm better off not living completely alone. But if he thinks I'm living in this madhouse, he's got another think coming. I will keep my room here as my art studio and reside in a very pleasant cottage on the estate. I've actually had my eye on one for a while. But that's between the two of us.

"Anyway, to the point. I will need an assistant of sorts. Someone to arrange engagements for me, drive me to meetings, order art supplies . . . that kind of thing. I am very particular about who enters my studios, but you and I would work well together, I think. It wouldn't be full-time, but I'd pay well and it would give you the time to be able to pick up your own artwork again."

"Oh, I wasn't planning to . . ."

Auntie Helena put a hand on Rose's arm. "You are a very talented artist, Rose. It would be a travesty if you didn't at least explore it a little further. If that's something you're interested in, of course?"

"It is," admitted Rose quietly. "Absolutely it is."

"And, of course, having you stay around has the added benefit of making my favourite nephew very happy," said Aunt Helena with a wink.

"There's nothing going on between Alastair and me," said Rose, quickly.

"Nothing going on *yet*," replied Aunt Helena with a wink. "Think about my offer." And with that, Aunt Helena wandered off to get a refill of her drink from Paul.

Rose looked around at the people in the room. She felt such affection for them all. Her eyes finally rested on Alastair who was laughing with his daughter. Imagine getting to stay here. To work for such a fantastic artist, and have time for her own artwork. And to see Alastair every day . . . Almost like he knew he was being watched, Alastair glanced up, caught her eye and smiled. Her stomach flipped. Did he like her? Like her, *like* her?

"He's very happy you stayed," said Mrs Reed, coming up next to her and indicating Alastair.

"Oh . . . um . . . well, it was really kind of everyone to invite me," said Rose.

"I think I was wrong to say what I did before. I'm protective over him, but it wasn't fair. You're not the sort to hurt him and you being here has been good for him, and for Isla." Mrs Reed smiled, patted Rose on the arm, before going to speak to Fiona. Rose was left rather red in the cheeks and swallowing hard. Had everyone been discussing her and Alastair apart from actually her and Alastair? Maybe it was time to do something about that . . .

Rose went over to the man himself, abandoned by Isla who had taken some treats out to Houdini who she fretted was missing out on all the fun. "I'm sure it must be my turn to choose a record now," she said.

"Are you certain? I think it's my turn." Rose pulled a face at him and looked through the choices.

"This one," she said, pulling out a copy of Henry Mancini's 'Moon River'. "It was my nan's favourite."

"A worthy choice," agreed Alastair. He took the record out of its sleeve and placed it on the turntable. The music began.

"Would you dance with me?" he asked, holding out his hand.

Rose looked around the room. "No one else is dancing."

"So?" said Alastair with a shrug. Rose took his hand. She was going to go along with whatever was happening here. There was absolutely no point to her trying to resist anyway. She was well beyond that.

There was a knock at the front door. "Just give me a minute," Alastair said, dropping her hand with a reluctant smile.

She watched him walk out of the room with butterflies in her stomach.

He returned a few minutes later, followed by Sarah and Lucy. Isla spotted her friend and went running over to hug her excitedly. The girls disappeared together.

"I'm so sorry to intrude," said Sarah to everyone. "We were on our way home and Lucy and I just thought it would be so lovely to wish a happy Christmas to you all."

It seemed Rose and Alastair were destined to be interrupted anytime they were even considering dancing together.

"Will you stay for a drink?" Alastair asked, hospitably.

"I suppose I'd better as I appear to have lost my daughter," Sarah said with an annoying, twinkly laugh.

Alastair took her over to where Paul was holding court, surrounded by cocktail-making ingredients.

"What's she doing here?" asked Fiona, coming over to speak with Rose.

"No idea," Rose said. "But it doesn't look like she's going to be in any hurry to leave."

* * *

An hour later and Sarah was still hanging around monopolising Alastair's company. Rose had been doing her best to ignore them and enjoy herself. She'd been looking forward to this evening and it would be a shame to spoil it because a boy she liked wasn't paying her attention. But she was so sad their dance had been spoiled yet again.

She carried a bunch of empty glasses out into the kitchen and was loading them in the dishwasher when Sarah and Alastair walked past the door. She heard Sarah say, "Oh, I absolutely insist you show me this Christmas tree. It sounds so vintage."

She managed to last about a minute before she couldn't bear it any longer. She had to know what was going on between those two. She came out of the kitchen and walked quietly through to the sitting room; its door was thankfully open.

She peered through the gap between the edge of the door and the doorframe.

"It's getting late," she heard Alastair say. "It'll be time for me to try to convince Isla to go to bed soon."

"Oh, she can stay up a bit longer, can't she?" Sarah replied. "It's Christmas, after all."

"Hi, Rose!" said Isla from behind her. "What on earth are you doing?"

Rose jumped and turned around to face Isla and Lucy who were both looking at her quizzically.

Before Rose could think up a plausible reply, she was saved by Alastair saying, "Just the daughter I wanted to see. I'm afraid it's time for you to be thrown out of this party, young lady."

Isla gave a dramatic sigh.

"I'm sure Lucy needs to be getting home as well," he added firmly.

"Oh, right, well, yes, I suppose so," said Sarah. She did not look best pleased. "I guess we'd better get our stuff together."

Rose made herself scarce while Sarah and Lucy left, not least because she was finding it hard to disguise the grin on her face. Surely there was no way that Alastair would be chucking Sarah out if he had any interest in her.

190

Conversely, he'd asked Rose to dance twice now as well as suggesting they go to get the yule log together . . . Not that that had turned out to be romantic in any way, shape or form, but still . . . And he wasn't her employer anymore. She was here as a guest.

* * *

Isla hung up her stocking and said good night to everyone before heading off to bed. The party reluctantly began to draw to a close with everyone knowing they'd be woken up early in the morning by overexcited children. Mrs Reed had to be stopped from helping with the cleaning and she and her husband left amid hugs and wishes for a merry Christmas.

Fiona, Paul and Aunt Helena said good night, leaving just Rose and Alastair downstairs emptying the dishwasher and hand-washing the delicate cocktail glasses.

Alastair sighed dramatically. "How come we're always the last ones standing when it comes to clearing up?"

"Must be because we're so good at it." Rose giggled.

"Do you think Isla will be asleep yet?"

"Probably not," said Rose. "I never used to sleep on Christmas Eve when I was a kid."

"I'll give her another few minutes and then I'll go and check."

"You know Fiona and Paul hid their presents in the wine cellar so they were able to retrieve them easily without potentially disturbing sleeping children. Why didn't we think of that?" muttered Rose.

"The wardrobe was your idea, if I recall," said Alastair.

"And it was a good idea . . . but the wine cellar is better."

Alastair snuck upstairs to check on Isla. "I think she's asleep," he proclaimed when he returned. "Shall we take our chance?"

"Absolutely," said Rose.

Alastair stopped. "Sorry, I think I just assumed we'd do this together." He ran his fingers through his hair. "It seems I have a habit of doing that . . ."

"It's fine. I'd like to help," Rose reassured.

They went upstairs and Rose opened the door to her room. They both walked in and Rose promptly pushed the door to behind them. Alastair raised an eyebrow comically, making Rose giggle. "In case Isla wakes up and comes out of her room," she whispered.

"Whatever you say . . ." said Alastair in such a way that it led to him being given a thump on the arm.

"Let's get these presents sorted out," said Rose, opening the wardrobe. "Why don't you take this one?" she said, turning around with a large present in her hand and finding herself facing Alastair's chest. She looked up and handed the present to him. "You're very tall, you know," she said, swallowing heavily.

"And you're very small," Alastair replied, huskily. His eyes locked with hers.

"Too small," Rose joked, not able to move her eyes from Alastair's.

"I actually think you're perfectly sized," Alastair said. He bent down slowly, never taking his eyes off hers until their lips were mere inches apart. He stopped, checking for her assent. Somehow, Rose managed to give the tiniest of nods and then, suddenly, he was kissing her with such intensity that it took her breath away.

The present landed on the ground between them with a soft thump as he pulled her to him, his hands strong against her waist. Rose's heart thumped wildly in her chest and she reached up and put her arms around his neck.

Rose felt Alastair falter suddenly.

"I thought I heard something," he said springing away from her. "Isla."

Rose listened and could indeed hear footsteps going down the stairs. Before she could say anything though, Alastair gave her an agonised look and hurried out of the room.

Rose was left alone in her bedroom feeling completely deflated. She waited a few minutes, allowing her breathing to calm and hoping that Alastair would return to her. When he didn't, she began carrying the presents downstairs — somebody had to and as they were in her bedroom, she wouldn't be able to go to sleep until they did. Plus, she didn't really know what else to do with herself.

The light in the hallway downstairs had been left on so Rose could see where she was going. As she reached the entrance hall and walked through to the sitting room, she saw the kitchen door had been pushed to. She could hear whispered voices from behind it. She hurried past, not wanting to be caught redhanded with the presents and wondering if it would be better to turn back. But she was almost at the sitting room now and knew Alastair wouldn't let Isla in there.

She smiled at the sight of the twins' stockings full to bursting even though she really felt like crying.

She didn't know why Alastair had kissed her, did he regret it now?

She'd been so looking forward to Christmas Day, and now she'd ruined it by kissing her boss. Or had he kissed her? The whole thing was a blur of lips and hands and . . . Okay, she needed to just get the presents under the tree so she could go up to bed and hopefully wake up realising the last half an hour had all been a dream.

She arranged the presents and headed back upstairs where Alastair was coming out of Isla's bedroom and softly closing the door behind him.

Rose took a deep breath before she asked quietly, "Is she okay?"

"Yeah," Alastair said. "She needed a glass of water and we got chatting . . . I'm sorry." He took a deep breath. "Um . . . about what happened before . . ."

"Paul's cocktails are lethal," said Rose as cheerfully as she could manage.

"Yeah . . ." Alastair looked like he was going to say more but Rose honestly couldn't face dealing with him continuing to try to let her down gently.

"Don't worry about it," she said with a shrug. "It's late so I started taking the presents downstairs . . ."

"Thanks, that was good of you. I can take over if you like."

"Great. The bag with all Isla's stocking gifts is right at the back of the wardrobe, under a blanket." said Rose, grateful for the excuse not to have to spend any more time with him. "I guess I'll take a quick shower then."

He didn't meet her eye. "I'll be done and out of your way before you're finished."

CHAPTER 19

Unfortunately when Rose woke up to the sounds of the twins calling out that Santa had been, she was acutely aware that what had happened the previous evening was not a dream and she now had to deal with the repercussions in front of rather a lot of people. What had happened? Had Alastair been drunk when he kissed her and then quickly realised the error of his ways? She recalled him trying to let her down gently. How embarrassing! She groaned and pulled the duvet over her head at the horror of the memory.

Could she get away with staying in bed? Ideally all day? Okay, that would probably be pushing things too far . . .

There was excited knocking on her door followed by James calling out, "Rose! Hurry! It's time to open presents!"

As much as she'd have liked to have remained where she was, she didn't want to upset the children and so Rose heaved herself out of bed and pulled on her dressing gown. It was almost 6 a.m., she supposed it could be worse.

Isla was waiting outside the room when Rose opened the door.

"Merry Christmas!" Isla said, her eyes sparkling.

"Have I got time to get dressed and sort out my hair?" Rose asked.

"Of course not!" Isla laughed. "It's Christmas Day! We always open up our presents in our pyjamas." Before Rose could protest, Isla had taken her hand and was leading her down the stairs.

* * *

Fiona and Alastair were making hot drinks for all the bleary-eyed adults in the kitchen.

"Don't worry, Rose! Coffee is on its way," called out Fiona.

"Thank goodness for that," muttered Aunt Helena, coming down the stairs behind Rose and not looking at all impressed by her early morning wake-up call. She did, however, manage to look glamorous even at this time of the day. She wore the most amazing dark green quilted dressing gown and there was a silk turban on her head. She made Rose feel even scruffier and she surreptitiously ran her fingers through her hair to tidy it up a bit. Rose's heart sank at the thought that she wouldn't be able to accept Aunt Helena's job offer after what had happened with Alastair. The realisation almost sent her running back to her room.

The family were gathering in the sitting room. The fire had been lit, there was still plenty of the yule log left as they hadn't left it burning overnight, and the Christmas tree lights had been turned on. It was the perfect homely Christmas scene.

The twins were sitting as patiently as possible, waiting for everyone to be in the room, their eyes roaming over the piles of presents under the tree, and in particular at the bulging stockings now on the floor in front of the fireplace.

Rose remembered feeling exactly the same way while waiting for her own mother to get a cup of tea and a biscuit on Christmas Day.

"Here we go," said Fiona, coming in, followed by Alastair carrying a large tray of drinks. "Let's see what's inside these stockings."

Rose averted her eyes from Alastair. She'd get through the day by staying out of his way as much as possible and concentrating on making sure Isla had a wonderful Christmas.

196

With whoops that made Aunt Helena sigh and close her eyes, the children tore into their stocking presents.

* * *

Twenty minutes later and most of what remained as evidence of all the hours spent wrapping was two bin bags full of discarded paper. Rose was pleased that everyone seemed to like their presents, especially Isla when she opened the hooped earrings for unpierced ears Rose had got her.

The last of the presents were being handed out and Rose was given one by Isla. "This is from me and my dad," she said.

Rose looked over at Alastair. She'd been steadfastly ignoring him, even when he was opening the socks covered with little pictures of Houdini she'd brought him and which had everyone in stitches. He was staring right back at her and gave a little nod towards the present.

Rose ripped through the paper to uncover a cardboard box. When she opened the lid she found a beautiful angel nestled in a pile of tissue paper. Lifting her out carefully, Rose put the box on the floor and held the angel in both hands. She was beautiful, antique but in immaculate condition with an intricately featured bone china face and gold wings and gown. She ran her fingers along her delicate wings, aware that she was still being watched.

"Thank you," she said, quietly, looking up to meet Alastair's eyes. He gave her a little smile.

"She's gorgeous." Fiona smiled.

"Do you like her?" asked Isla, excitedly, drawing Rose's attention to her. "Is she just like the one your mum had on her tree?"

"I love her," said Rose. "And she's a little fancier than the one my mum had!" She must have cost a lot, Rose knew.

"Can I put her on top of the tree?" Isla asked.

Rose turned to Alastair to check if this was all right and he gave her a little nod. "Be really careful," Alastair warned.

"I will be, Dad," reassured Isla.

"Wait a minute, I'll get you a step," Alastair said. Isla gave a not very subtle roll of her eyes but waited until her father returned and placed a step in front of the Christmas tree. Isla climbed up and replaced the star with the angel.

"That looks a lot better," declared James.

"Agreed," said Aunt Helena. "Who knew my nephew could be so thoughtful and had such good taste."

Rose felt herself blushing and wished the ground would just open up to swallow her.

"Who wants some breakfast?" asked Fiona. "I'll get some bacon on."

Murmurs of assent were followed by tired grown-ups forcing themselves out of their seats.

"Can I do anything to help?" Rose asked.

"Thank you, but don't worry. It's all under control," Fiona assured. "Why don't you take half an hour for yourself? I know all of us together can be a little much," she joked.

"It's lovely being with you all, but maybe I will go and get dressed and sort my hair out a bit," Rose said.

"Would you like a chocolate coin, Rose?" offered Isla.

"I would love one, thank you," Rose said, accepting the chocolate.

"I'm so glad you're here with us, Rose," Isla said, spontaneously hugging her. "This is the best Christmas ever."

Rose's heart melted as she hugged Isla back. She could put up with a little awkwardness when she was around Alastair if it meant Isla had a good Christmas. How on earth had Isla's mother managed to desert this wonderful child? Rose was going to find it hard enough going back to London soon and she'd only known Isla for a few weeks. But she'd think about that after Christmas. She had enough to occupy her mind today.

* * *

Rose got dressed, put on some make-up and brushed her hair. It was good to have a few minutes alone to clear her mind and figure out how she was going to get through the day. Of course her mind went straight to the kiss . . . She didn't think she'd ever been kissed with such ferocity before. It was like he yearned for her, but then . . . She shook her head. What was the point in going over it? Alastair had made his feelings completely clear.

But he'd got her such a thoughtful present. Did that mean anything? No, she told herself firmly. She needed to stop with this. Alastair told her he didn't date and he'd made it clear he didn't want her getting close to Isla. Last night had just been a moment of craziness brought on by Christmas and alcohol which he'd obviously regretted immediately.

* * *

She checked herself in the mirror and steeled her resolve before returning back downstairs.

"Perfect timing," said Fiona when Rose entered the kitchen. The children were already sitting at the island eating their breakfast. Her sous chef, Paul, handed Rose a plate of bacon, scrambled eggs and toast.

"Thank you," said Rose, as she took a seat next to James. "This looks great."

The back door opened and Alastair came in with the dogs.

"Do not let them shake mud all over the kitchen," Fiona warned. Both dogs promptly gave a good shake.

"You're cleaning that up," muttered Fiona, handing Alastair a plate of food.

"As soon as I've eaten this," he promised. He glanced at the empty seat next to Rose, but seemed to think better of it, and sat at the table, where he was soon joined by Aunt Helena.

The children left; Isla was going to put on some cartoons for her cousins before taking her new bike out on the driveway.

"What time are Sarah and Lucy arriving?" Fiona asked her brother once the children were out of hearing, making Rose's ears prick up.

"I said we'd be eating at three but that they should feel free to come earlier if they liked," Alastair replied.

"I wish you'd spoken to me about inviting them . . ." grumbled Fiona in a way that was most unlike her.

"We've got plenty of food for two more, and Isla will love having her friend here."

Fiona shrugged and tried to catch Rose's eye.

Rose's heart sank. She couldn't believe that today was about to get even harder. How could she sit through yet another session of Sarah flirting with Alastair? But what choice did she have? She could hardly spoil Isla's Christmas by excusing herself.

* * *

Sarah and Lucy turned up an hour later in bright Christmas jumpers and bearing wine and chocolates.

Rose stayed in the kitchen peeling potatoes for as long as she politely could before heading into the entrance hall to greet them.

"Oh, you're still here," Sarah said, spotting Rose.

"I am." Rose forced a welcoming smile onto her face. "I was very kindly invited to stay for Christmas."

Sarah's face fell for a moment but she quickly corrected it. "Isn't Alastair just the best, taking in us refugees?" She gave Alastair's arm a squeeze.

"We all invited Rose actually," said Fiona, loyally. "We decided we couldn't possibly have Christmas without her."

"How sweet," said Sarah, absentmindedly. "Alastair, sweetie? Time for a holiday drinkie?"

"It's 10 a.m.," commented Aunt Helena with a fantastically judgmental tone as she came down the stairs.

"Actually," said Paul, skilfully, "The turkey's just gone in the oven and we were going to head out for a walk with the dogs. There are plenty of wellies you can borrow if you didn't bring any with you."

Sarah's face sank but Lucy looked thrilled. "Can Houdini come as well?" she asked.

"Of course," cried Isla. "We wouldn't leave him out! Come on, we'll find you and your mum some wellies. You might want to borrow some clothes from me as well because it's going to be really muddy."

Everyone dispersed to get ready, Sarah sticking with Alastair.

Rose slipped into the sitting room and set about tidying it up a little bit after the present opening excitement of earlier. She smiled at the tree; it really did look beautiful, and absolutely right for the room. She was so happy that everyone liked it.

"Are you okay?" Fiona asked, coming into the room. The sympathy on her face left Rose in no doubt that Fiona knew she was hiding.

"Yeah," said Rose, brightly. "Just a headache. I thought I'd just check in here and then have a little lie down while you're out . . ." Isla had her friend with her now, she wouldn't notice when Rose didn't join the group.

"If you're sure."

"I am. I'll feel much brighter by the time you get back."

"Okay." Fiona gave Rose a hug. "I'll see you in a bit."

"Do you need me to check on the turkey while you're out?"

"It'll be fine, don't worry."

Fiona left and Rose continued putting the room straight. She heard everyone reconvene and sighed as the front door closed. An hour or so of peace would help her come up with a plan of action for getting through this day now that Sarah was in the equation. One that didn't involve the bottles of prosecco chilling in the fridge.

She couldn't believe she'd got herself into this situation. She should be having an amazing Christmas in this beautiful house with new friends and considering the offer of potentially a really great job, but she just had to mess things up by kissing her boss. The best-looking man she'd ever met. And probably the kindest. And funniest. And sweetest. Especially when he was with Isla.

If it had just been a misjudged, drunken kiss, she'd be better able to deal with it by laughing off and putting it behind them. But that wasn't what it had felt like, not at all. It felt like there was meaning being that kiss, like they'd been building up to it and were finally able to give in to what they both wanted. Or, at least, that's how it had felt to her. But, of course, she was wrong. First, he couldn't get away fast enough and then he invited Sarah for Christmas. He couldn't have made it clearer that he wasn't interested in her.

Why did she have to fall in love with her boss? Because, of course, that's exactly what she'd stupidly gone and done. And who could blame her really? Alastair was, well, perfect.

"There you are," said Alastair's voice from behind her, making her jump because she'd been so deep in her thoughts about him. She blushed as she turned to face him, wondering if he suspected what she'd been thinking about.

"I thought you were out walking the dogs with everyone," she said as lightly as she could manage.

"Fiona said you were staying behind and I wanted to check you're all right."

"I'm fine," said Rose, quickly. "Just a little stomach ache."

"Fiona said you had a headache . . ."

"Yes . . . a headache . . . that's what I meant," said Rose, weakly.

"I wanted to talk to you . . . about last night." He looked supremely uncomfortable. "I know you said we didn't need to, but I should apologise . . ."

"Really, it's fine," Rose muttered, quickly. She turned to leave, but he stopped her, gently placing a hand on her arm.

"Please can we discuss it?"

"Okay. Well, it was obviously a mistake . . ."

"Was it?" asked Alastair, gently.

"Yes . . . I mean, I never would have . . . if I'd realised that you and Sarah . . ." She was doing everything she could

202

to avoid making eye contact with him, knowing that would be her undoing and would likely lead to her making an even bigger fool of herself than she already had.

"There's nothing going on between Sarah and I. She's here today because her oven broke down and they didn't have anywhere else to go for Christmas dinner. I'm not interested in Sarah. I'd hoped she'd got that message loud and clear by now."

"Oh, right," said Rose, "Then . . ."

"I kissed you because I couldn't stop myself," continued Alastair. "But, first of all, I'm your boss and I didn't want you to think I was trying to take advantage of you . . ."

"Technically, you're not my boss. Not anymore," pointed out Rose.

"That's true . . ."

"You didn't take advantage of me," said Rose. "But you also don't date."

"I don't," confirmed Alastair, making her heart sink. "Because I've had my heart trampled on and I honestly hadn't found anyone I trusted enough to want to date . . . until now. But, of course, you don't date either . . ."

"True. Though I'm perfectly willing to change my mind. For the right person. But you left . . ."

"Isla . . ."

"Right . . ."

"Who actually set me straight on a few things," Alastair said, gently.

"She did?" Rose looked up and they locked eyes. Damn.

"Yep, she saw me coming out of your room and quizzed me in her inimitable way . . . She was kind of mad that I'd left you . . ."

"Good old Isla." Rose laughed.

"As soon as I knew she was fine, happy actually, for us to be together, I came back to find you, but . . ."

"I thought you regretted kissing me . . ."

"And you said it was a drunken mistake."

"I don't regret kissing you, Rose."

"And I wasn't drunk."

They smiled shyly at each other.

"I wanted to give you your Christmas present," Alastair said.

"I thought the angel was my present," Rose said, glancing up at her beautiful gift sitting proudly on top of the Christmas tree.

"I've got another present for you, but I didn't want to give it to you in front of everyone else." Alastair walked over to a cupboard and took out a large box with a bow on it.

He handed it to Rose who placed it down on the table and lifted the lid. She let out a little gasp as she pulled out the dress she'd worn to the Christmas event.

"You looked so incredibly beautiful wearing it. It's meant to be yours."

"But it must have cost a fortune!"

"Let's just make sure you get plenty of use out of it then," said Alastair.

"It's hardly the sort of dress I'd wear around the house."

"You can if you like," Alastair said with a grin. "As long as it's around this house."

Rose opened her mouth to speak, but Alastair placed a finger lightly on her lips.

"Don't go back to London," he said.

"But . . ."

"Stay here. With me. And Isla."

Rose was too shocked, too delighted, to say anything.

"Aunt Helena told me about the job she's offered you . . ."

"That was very kind of her," Rose said.

"You'd be really good at it and I think you'd enjoy it. And it would give you time for your own artwork. Plus, my aunt may not like people very much, but she has a lot of connections in the art world, as does my sister, so they're useful people to know."

"Yes, but . . ."

"If it's staying in this house that's the problem, I have a cottage on the estate you'd be more than welcome to use if you'd prefer."

"It's not the house, I love this house, you know that . . ."

"What is it then?" asked Alastair gently.

Rose took a deep breath before saying, "What about Isla? I know how worried you are about her thinking of me as a mother figure . . ."

"I told you, Isla adores you," said Alastair. "As do I. And I know you'd never intentionally hurt us. Isla set me straight on that, and she was completely right. I was hurt once and shut myself off, but you are nothing like Marie. If at some point in the future you'd like to be a mother figure to her, I can't think of anything either of us would love more."

"Are you sure?" Rose asked, not daring to believe Alastair's words as she looked up into his green eyes.

"I have never been more sure of anything in my life. You've completely bewitched me, and if you'll have me, I'm yours. I love you, Rose. I think I've been a little bit in love with you ever since I handed you back your tiara, and I'm just falling deeper."

"I love you, too," whispered Rose. If she was honest with herself, she'd realised that even before they'd kissed.

Alastair took her chin gently in his hand and tilted it up. "Would you look at that? We're right under the mistletoe . . ."

"How very convenient," Rose breathed, as Alastair pulled her into his arms and kissed her.

"This is the best Christmas ever," murmured Rose.

"I couldn't sleep last night thinking about that kiss," Alastair admitted. "I thought I'd completely messed things up . . . but I couldn't not tell you how I feel."

"I'm so glad you did," said Rose reaching up to touch the side of Alastair's face.

"Rose! Lucy's mum fell in a cow poo and had to go home to change," Isla called out as she came running into the sitting room, closely followed by the rest of the family. "Oh!"

Rose flushed bright red and attempted to hide her face in Alastair's jumper. He laughed and kissed the top of her head, before gently turning her around to face everyone.

Isla looked absolutely ecstatic.

"I'm hoping this means you'll be accepting my job offer," said Aunt Helena looking rather smug.

"If it's still available," Rose said.

"It is," confirmed Aunt Helena.

"Then I'd like to accept it very much and stay here," said Rose.

Alastair turned to face his aunt. "You're going to move here?"

"Into the empty cottage by the bothy. I'll have an architect send you the plans so work can get started," Aunt Helena replied.

"That all sounds really good to me," Alastair said, his face breaking into a grin.

"Bahhhhhh!" came an indignant bleat.

"How on earth did you get in here?" asked Rose, grabbing Houdini by the collar before he could eat the Christmas tree.

Houdini went to nibble on Rose's jeans.

"Oh no, you don't," said Alastair, taking over from Rose. "Rose is all mine."

EPILOGUE

Just over two years later...

The weather outside was typical of a January evening in Edinburgh: freezing cold and raining, but inside the gallery it was warm and bright and alive with the hum of people milling around, champagne flutes in hands, and enjoying the watercolour collection on display.

Rose walked about the exhibition taking in the atmosphere and attempting to be as surreptitious as possible. There was plenty of champagne left, she noted, and canapés were circling — once you'd worked in events, she supposed you never stopped checking things were running smoothly.

"You've done beautifully, my dear," said Aunt Helena from next to her. Aunt Helena looked resplendent in a bright pink kaftan and was obviously in her element.

"Do you really think so?" Rose asked.

"I do. Have you seen how many sold stickers there are already? I don't think I sold a single piece from my first exhibition."

Rose raised an eyebrow.

"All right, maybe I did sell one or two," Aunt Helena admitted.

"I bet you didn't have a mentor who organised your first exhibition in one of the most famous galleries in the UK," Rose commented.

"Believe me, they didn't need much persuading. Your work is exceptional."

"Thank you!" Rose surprised Aunt Helena with a hug. "I can't believe I have a collection and that people have come and are interested in seeing it!"

"I have absolutely no trouble believing this," said Alastair, coming up behind Rose and putting his arms around her. "Are you okay?" he whispered into her hair.

"I think so," she murmured. "I feel better with you here."

"It looks amazing," he assured her. "I'm so proud of you."

A waiter came over. "Would you like a drink?" Alastair asked, helping himself to a glass of champagne from the offered tray.

"No, thanks. I should keep a clear head," Rose said.

"There she is!" Isla appeared from the crowds, followed by her aunt and uncle.

"Thank you all so much for coming," Rose said as she found herself surrounded. She couldn't stop smiling. This evening was like a dream come true. A dream she'd tucked away for so long, sure that it was out of reach. She just wished her mother could be there.

"Excuse me? Rose?" said a young man carrying a dictaphone. "I'm Rob Harrow, from the *Edinburgh Tribune*. Have you got a minute to answer some questions for a piece about this evening?"

"Sure!" Rose tried not to show how nervous she was.

"We'll leave you to it, and catch up later," said Fiona, kissing Rose on the cheek, and leading her husband and Aunt Helena away to go and look around the exhibition.

"Great! Well, first of all, is it okay for me to call you Rose or do you prefer Lady Rose now that you're a laird's wife?"

Rose laughed. "Rose is fine!"

"And you're supported by your husband tonight?"

"She is," said Alastair. "I wouldn't have missed this for anything."

"And her daughter!" said Isla, anxious not to be left out.

Rose put her arm around Isla. "That's right."

"Mum properly adopted me last month," Isla announced, sounding so proud. "She's the best mum ever."

Rose wondered if she would ever stop feeling emotional when Isla called her mum; she suspected not. Especially when she recalled the look on Isla's face when she unwrapped her completed adoption papers on Christmas Day.

She felt Alastair taking her hand in his and giving it a little squeeze.

"Wow, congratulations," said the reporter. "And this is your first exhibition?"

"It is," said Rose. "And it's dedicated to the memory of my mother, Elaine Alridge. It's a collection based on the things she loved most. Her favourite landscapes, people, buildings, flowers. Anything that I remember she loved, I have included."

"What a wonderful memorial."

"I hope so," Rose said. She could feel tears pricking her eyes.

"My wife needs to mingle with her guests now, but if you have any more questions, I'm sure she'll be more than happy to answer them if you want to call or arrange a meeting," said Alastair, smoothly. "Let me give you a contact number."

"Thank you," Rose mouthed as the journalist left.

"Not a problem. Isla, would you mind going to check with Aunt Fiona that everything's set up with the microphone?"

Isla gave a salute and set off in search of her aunt.

Alastair turned to his wife. "It's nearly time for you to give your speech. Are you sure you don't want a little Dutch courage?"

"I would," Rose said, "But I can't."

"I can get you one . . ." Alastair looked around for a waiter.

"No, I can't because I'm pregnant," she said, completely failing to hide her massive grin until she'd finished her announcement.

209

"Pregnant?" Alastair whispered. "Rose! Oh, wow!"

"Are you pleased?"

"Are you kidding me?" he said beaming, pulling her gently into a hug. "I'm thrilled, absolutely thrilled."

"And do you think Isla will be happy? I don't want her to think she's being usurped . . . We had said we'd wait a little while . . ."

"She is going to love having a little brother or sister to boss around. Can we tell her this evening?"

"Yes, but shall we wait until we get home?"

"That sounds like a great idea. That way she can let Houdini know straight away too." Alastair rolled his eyes.

"You know I caught him in the pantry again this morning. I don't know how he does it!"

"He's a nightmare, but he's Isla's nightmare."

"He is indeed," said Rose.

"Come on then my ridiculously talented wife. Let's get your speech out of the way and then you can relax and properly enjoy your special evening. We've got a lot of celebrating to do."

"I couldn't have done any of this without you."

"I didn't do anything," said Alastair, gently.

"Yes, you did. You, and Isla, and Mrs Reed, and Aunt Helena and Fiona and Paul, and even Houdini I suppose. You brought me back to life. Without you, I'm not sure I would have ever returned to art."

"I'm very happy for any tiny, miniscule part I played in this exhibition," Alastair said, "But the talent and the hard work is all down to you."

"I love you," said Rose, reaching up to kiss him.

"And I love you," Alastair replied, holding her close. 'So very much.'

THE END

THE JOFFE BOOKS STORY

We began in 2014 when Jasper agreed to publish his mum's much-rejected romance novel and it became a bestseller.

Since then we've grown into the largest independent publisher in the UK. We're extremely proud to publish some of the very best writers in the world, including Joy Ellis, Faith Martin, Caro Ramsay, Helen Forrester, Simon Brett and Robert Goddard. Everyone at Joffe Books loves reading and we never forget that it all begins with the magic of an author telling a story.

We are proud to publish talented first-time authors, as well as established writers whose books we love introducing to a new generation of readers.

We won Trade Publisher of the Year at the Independent Publishing Awards in 2023. We have been shortlisted for Independent Publisher of the Year at the British Book Awards for the last four years, and were shortlisted for the Diversity and Inclusivity Award at the 2022 Independent Publishing Awards. In 2023 we were shortlisted for Publisher of the Year at the RNA Industry Awards.

We built this company with your help, and we love to hear from you, so please email us about absolutely anything bookish at feedback@joffebooks.com

If you want to receive free books every Friday and hear about all our new releases, join our mailing list: www.joffebooks.com

And when you tell your friends about us, just remember: it's pronounced Joffe as in coffee or toffee!